The Wish King

K. S. Gerlt

Wishes make a great servant, but a terrible master.

1

Orion

I swung my sword in a practiced arc, the blade whistling as it sliced through the air. Sweat beaded on my brow, and my muscles ached with soreness, but I relished the strain. Every spare moment I had, I poured into some manner of training, whether with the sword or with magic.

I had been unable to sit still ever since the witches had attacked the Druid Queen's seat of power in Pyrcairn, interrupting our alliance talks and the revelation that Astrid was actually the Druid Queen's long-lost niece, and the rightful Druid Princess.

Every time I closed my eyes, however, I was haunted by the memory of how Adelaide, the witch that Astrid and I had trusted, had betrayed us. Not only had she sold us out to the

Headwitch of the Redgraves in the hopes of regaining her lost honor and sealed powers, but she had also abandoned Rafe, her wolf-druid companion and the son of Queen Rowena, in order to kidnap Astrid.

My heart ached just thinking about it.

Much had happened in an incredibly short time, but we would only get busier from here on out. And if I kept dwelling on the look in Astrid's eyes as she was held hostage, suspended in the air by Adelaide's magic...I would either be paralyzed with regret or blinded by rage.

I had spent the last several days in strategy meetings with Queen Rowena, Captain Jolene, Rafe, and Commander Regis, of Harland. Now, instead of simply retaking Astoria from Nyra and her desert invaders, we also needed to rescue Astrid—before it was too late. The curse of corruption Astrid had re-activated in order to save my life when Nyra tried to kill me was quickly eating away at her magic. If we could not get to her soon, I could lose her forever.

Although I had gifted Astrid the precious star-shaped necklace my mother had crafted for me, which could grant one single wish, I had no way to know if she had used it. Even if she did, I feared the magic it contained would not be enough to dispel a curse that a fallen star could not. And that meant I needed to somehow learn how to use my own magic before I returned—just in case.

Simple.

I sighed, and ran a hand through my dark hair. Noctus glanced at me from where he was lounging in the sitting room of my guest suite, sharpening his favorite blades. He always did that when he was anxious or worried. I got out my own whetstone and sat down beside him to do the same.

"We will get her back." Noctus' voice was quiet, but firm.

"But what if we are too late?" I whispered hoarsely.

Noctus paused, setting down his whetstone. His dark, solemn eyes met mine. "Then we avenge her."

His words felt like a dagger through my heart. I swallowed, but managed to nod around the lump that rose in my throat. I did not even want to *consider* that possibility. If I did, I was afraid I might come undone at the seams.

"I believe Rafe was right in his assessment, however—they will keep her alive as long as they can, to use as bait. Adelaide knows that stardust buys Astrid time, so I doubt it will come to that." He curled his lip when he said the witch's name, as if it left a bad taste in his mouth.

"You are right." I blew out a breath. "Thank you, Noctus. For sticking with me through everything."

He gave me a rare smile. "Though darkness falls..."

"Still the stars find their way," I answered. Then I gave a shaky laugh. "I am eternally grateful *you* were the one who picked my pocket all those years ago."

Noctus' smile widened. "As am I."

Then he held up his hand, and I realized with a start that he had snatched my starsteel watch without my noticing. Again. I laughed. "Still got it, I see."

"I like to keep my skills sharp. Never know when they might come in handy." Just as he held out my watch to me, it began to glow, signifying I had received a new message.

I quickly took it from him and snapped the lid open, my eyes skimming quickly over the glowing letters etched in starlight on the underside of the lid. "Rigel is reporting that things have taken a turn for the worse back home, but that that has made it easier to recruit more people to our side."

"Does he know...?" Noctus trailed off.

I grimaced. "Not yet. I completely forgot to update him on the events of the last week."

My fingers flew across the face of the watch as I drew the letters, the buzzing energy of the starlight turning my hair silver. I briefly summarized the attack and its consequences, including Astrid's abduction and our newly-secured alliances with the druids, the starship captains, and Harland. Plus, I asked him to keep an eye out for any witch activity.

I did not have to wait long for his response.

"He says he will have his spies search for where they are keeping Astrid. If he could free her, that would be ideal, but I doubt Nyra will make it that easy for us," I informed Noctus. "He will also begin making preparations to conceal, house, and supply our incoming allies."

Noctus nodded. "We will need to put all of our safehouses into use, plus those of our allies."

I grimaced as I read his following message. "He is hinting none-too-subtly that recruiting would be easier if the people had a figure to rally behind."

Allowing everyone to believe Nyra's lies, that she had killed me alongside my father, had been what was best at the time. I had needed time to heal—from my physical wounds, as well as from my mental ones. Such absolute betrayal had left scars in me that I doubted would ever fully heal.

But now that I had made allies out of the neighboring kingdoms, I no longer had an excuse to delay the inevitable. Besides, I was running out of time if I wanted to save Astrid.

Noctus set a hand on my shoulder. "It is time."

I clenched my jaw, then took a fortifying breath. Noctus was right. It was now or never. I just hoped that by the time this was all over, everyone I cared about was still standing by my side, unhurt.

I wrote out my message and showed it to Noctus before I sent it. He grinned, and clapped me on the shoulder.

"Prince Sterling is officially back among the living. Congratulations. That rumor will spread like wildfire."

"Good to be back." I sent the starnote and smiled at the excited answer Rigel sent back.

"I imagine you just made Rigel's job much easier." Noctus chuckled.

"And Nyra's much harder."

"Hopefully, her patrols will be shooting at ghosts long before we arrive." Noctus' tone darkened.

"I think I will have Rigel make sure of it," I mused, an idea forming in my mind. I sent off one more instruction, one that I hoped would help turn the tide in our favor. We would need every possible advantage if we were going to pull this off successfully, with minimal casualties.

A lump rose in my throat when I read his response. "Rigel promises to do all that he can, and that we will save Astrid—no matter what it takes."

I wrote back, *Let our fathers be the last people she steals from us.*

Long live King Sterling, was his only reply.

2

Astrid

When my vision cleared, it took me a minute to realize that Headwitch Brunhilde had taken us to Astoria, instead of to the mountains the Redgrave Coven called home. We were in some kind of garden courtyard, surrounded by soaring stone walls patrolled by armed soldiers. I had not known the witches were capable of traveling great distances in an instant like this.

My chest ached, both from the magic binding me and from the horror of what had just happened. Moments ago, I had been in the Druidlands with Orion and my long-lost aunt, Queen Rowena, fighting off an attack by the witches. Adelaide had betrayed me, betrayed us *all*, and taken me hostage to use against Orion. But amidst all of the confusion, the witch had taken *me* with her when she teleported away, instead of Orion. My blood boiled as my fear and helplessness turned to fury.

When Adelaide's attention shifted, the magic bindings that held me loosened, and I took the opportunity to strike her.

"Traitor," I hissed. "And to think I defended you! I should have let Jolene throw you overboard!"

"Perhaps you should have." I frowned at her cold response.

She kept her face carefully blank, even as she rewove and tightened the bindings until I could hardly breathe, let alone move.

My eyes widened as I saw the Headwitch slap her hard across the face. Adelaide was sent reeling. Despite her outwardly thin and almost frail appearance, Headwitch Brunhilde seemed abnormally strong.

"For once, I find myself agreeing with a druid." The hag curled her lip in disgust at Adelaide. "He was right in front of you! How could you possibly *miss?!*"

Adelaide slowly righted her head to stare at me in confusion. I glared at her defiantly, trying and failing to speak around the magical gag in my mouth. Why *had* she taken me?

"It will be at least another *day* before I can cast a port spell again!" the Headwitch continued to rage. "But by then, he could be gone!" She rounded on Adelaide, her hand raised. "I will be resealing your magic, and you will never leave your den again! There is nothing you could possibly do to make up for this failure! You are even more *useless* than your hopeless mother!"

"He will come to us!" Adelaide cringed, waiting for the blow to fall. I noticed she braced, but did not try to defend herself.

"What do you mean?"

"The prince is in love with her—with Astrid," she explained hastily, gesturing to me. I gasped in outrage. "And he knows we have her now. He will come to save her."

"You set a trap." The Headwitch lowered her hand, peering at her through squinted eyes. "With his lover as bait."

"Yes, Headwitch," she rushed on as the hag's sneer slowly turned into a wicked grin. "There is no need to seek him out; he will come to us, and the Redgraves will have the magic of a fallen star at our disposal."

I went pale and began to flail angrily against the magic binding me. *No!* I refused to be used against Orion like this! This was *exactly* the sort of situation I had been trying so hard to *avoid!* But the Headwitch only grinned down at me with her yellow, rotting teeth.

"So long as he appears before this one expires..." she cackled, "I will be the most powerful witch of all. And *you* will have finally made up for your disgrace of a mother."

Adelaide bowed her head. "Thank you, Headwitch."

"Come." She turned on her heel and marched through the courtyard, grinning wickedly at anyone who dared to so much as look her way.

Adelaide followed behind, and floated me in front of her so she could keep an eye on me. Not that I could do much.

As we moved through the castle, I noticed that almost every person we passed was a tribesman, armed to the teeth with weapons and brimming with magic. The few Astorians I saw kept their heads down. Anytime a tribesman walked by, they would move out of the way and bow, a motion that went largely ignored by the armed thugs. The halls were quiet, except for the shuffling of boots on stone. No one spoke. No one laughed.

It had only been two months or so since the Woman-King conducted her silent invasion, but the Astorians seemed thoroughly beaten.

We paraded through the grand halls, up several staircases, and around to a large audience chamber within the castle's keep that was guarded by a cadre of tribesmen. It had high, arched ceilings with skylights cut into it, so we could see the stars, and they could see us. Oil paintings and suits of armor lined the walls, all of them forged of starsteel. A grand rug carpeted the stone floor, but based on the indents in it, I could tell that a large, round meeting table had been removed. Instead, a large golden throne now dominated the far end of the room.

And in it lounged the Woman-King.

The tribeswoman frowned as we approached, her eyes narrowing in anger when she spotted me. I glared right back at the snake wearing human skin.

"My request was for the fugitive Sterling. Not his pathetic healer." Her voice was warm and rich, in stark contrast to her expression and words. It grated on my ears.

Headwitch Brunhilde dipped her head, a sight that surprised me. Witches were prideful creatures, and *never* bowed to humans. Even humans with magic. "The Redgrave coven has greatly weakened the druids, with whom the fugitive was seeking an alliance."

"And what does that matter to me?" She peered down her nose at the hag, whose chin quivered in anger for a breath.

"Before we were forced to retreat, my apprentice captured the boy's lover, who also just so happens to be the druids' princess." She gestured grandly at me. "And we have reason to believe the fugitive will come here willingly, in a foolish attempt to free her."

Nyra narrowed her eyes thoughtfully, in a way that reminded me of a predator. "That *does* sound like something that fool would do."

"We will be able to capture the fugitive and many of his allies in one fell swoop, with minimal expenditures on our part." Headwitch Brunhilde cackled while rubbing her dry hands together gleefully.

"The Redgraves have proven most worthy of their reward. Should your plan succeed, I am prepared to offer the Redgraves a commission for the largest hex ever cast, and a reward to match." The Woman-King smiled at the Headwitch indulgently, like a mother dangling sweets before her child.

It worked; I could see the excited twitch of her nose, and the way she licked her cracked lips. I felt the blood drain from my face. What new evil was Nyra concocting that required the help of the witches beyond their use as soldiers and executioners?

Perhaps it was a blessing in disguise that I was here. If I could learn what that traitor was planning and somehow get a message back to Orion—or even to Rigel... I might be more useful to Orion as his spy than as his healer.

I grunted in pain as I was roughly thrown into a dungeon cell. My knees scraped against the uneven stone floor, my gauzy dress doing little to protect the skin. I tried to break my fall with my arms, but it was difficult since they were still bound together by Adelaide's magic.

"I must alert the rest of the coven immediately. Join me when you are finished here." Headwitch Brunhilde's cruel grin left little doubt as to what she expected Adelaide to do to me.

"Yes, Headwitch." Adelaide bobbed her head respectfully as the old hag bustled away.

Adelaide closed the iron cell door, locking it with a key one of the gruff tribesmen handed to her. I glared daggers at her from my dark cell, since magic still wrapped around my mouth like a gag. The flickering torch light from the hallway did little to illuminate the area or ward off the damp chill that seemed to seep into my very bones.

With a flick of her wrist, she removed the magic gagging me and binding my hands and ankles. I noticed she was purposefully avoiding my eyes.

"How could you betray us like this?!" I yelled the moment the gag faded. I wanted answers from her.

She gave no response.

The sting of her betrayal was a living thing inside my chest, made all the more painful by the knowledge that without *my* insistence on giving her a chance, Captain Jolene and Orion would not have allowed her to stay. I had pitied her, felt empathy for a girl whose story so closely mirrored my own.

This was all my fault.

My only consolation was that *I* had been taken, instead of *Orion*. He was still back in the Druidlands with my aunt, working on securing alliances to help him retake Astoria. Orion was still free to do what needed to be done.

I rubbed my wrists sullenly, trying to work some feeling back into them. I tried to ignore the darkened veins there that signified how much damage the curse was doing. My bow and dagger had been confiscated, along with my pouch of stardust. At least they had not discovered the star pendant Orion had given me, which I kept tucked beneath my dress. Why Adelaide had not reported it remained a mystery to me.

Adelaide turned to leave, the tribesmen filtering out before her.

Changing tactics, I said quietly, "Nyra has already betrayed Orion and the former Chieftains of the Talahari Desert Tribes in her quest for power. Not to mention how little regard she has for the lives of witches. What makes you think she will not betray *you*, as well?"

Adelaide paused, her shoulders stiffening.

"And if you are such a useful little tool to your Headwitch, what makes you think she would ever keep her word and unseal your magic? Especially after you captured *the wrong person?*"

The witch half-turned, a flicker of anger, but also of uncertainty, flitting through her crimson eyes.

"Shut your mouth! You have no idea what it has been like for me."

"Oh, but I do. I was cursed by my own grandfather and cast out of the Druidlands for the crime of being *born*. My magic was sealed, just like yours, and I was abused and nearly sold into slavery before Orion rescued me. But unlike you, I am going to *die, alone in a dank dungeon, far from everyone I love.* But please, tell me again how bad you have it," I hissed.

Adelaide scowled. Her mouth opened and closed like a fish's, as if she were trying to find a retort but came up empty.

"I *vouched* for you. I welcomed you into our cobbled-together family. But instead of starting a *new* life with people who actually *value* you, with or *without* your magic, you decided to follow in Nyra's footsteps. You betrayed us. And you even betrayed and abandoned Rafe, too." All of my anger and pain cascaded from my tongue like a venomous waterfall, but it did little to alleviate the burning heat of my emotions.

Adelaide whirled around, clenching her hands into fists. Reddish magic gathered around them, casting the sneer on her face into sharp relief.

"Do not speak his name!" she yelled, raising her magic-wreathed hands towards me.

My eyes widened, and fear shot through me. Was she really about to hex me? Any hex she cast would only fuel the curse, giving it more magic to consume and shortening whatever time I had left. But then, a strange sense of calm floated over me, muting my riotous emotions.

Would it really be such a bad thing if the curse ran its course? Then this horrible ride of ups and downs, of hope and despair, would be over. And Nyra would no longer have her bait. Orion would be free to focus on retaking and rebuilding his kingdom.

"Do it!" I screamed, half-rising from where I sat on the floor.

Just then, the curse roared to life, and darkness licked at the edges of my vision. I coughed violently as I fell back, my chest heaving for air. A tear slipped down my cheek as stabbing pain covered my body, unrelenting needles that danced over every inch of skin.

I curled into a ball as I fought to stay conscious and ride out the waves of agony that threatened to drown me. I reached for my pouch of stardust before remembering it was no longer there. Instead, I clenched my hand into a fist and bit down on it, refusing to give Adelaide the satisfaction of hearing me scream.

After what felt like a small eternity, the pain receded like the tide, leaving me panting and gasping for breath. Sweat beaded on my skin, and the cold air swept in to send chills down my spine.

But to my surprise, instead of appearing triumphant, Adelaide stood over me with a haunted look on her face. The magic had dissipated from her hands, which trembled slightly as she held them out before her. She stared at them, and then at me, as if she did not recognize either one.

"Nice try," she whispered hoarsely. She ran a shaking hand through her hair, as if trying to compose herself. "But you will remain alive—as *bait*—until that soft-hearted prince comes looking for you."

I gritted my teeth, which had already begun to chatter. So she had realized I was goading her. I felt both disappointed and relieved. I attempted to get to my feet, to argue some more, but my arms gave out. After that last attack, I was too exhausted to move, and too tired and weak to think of anything else to say.

Without another word, Adelaide turned and left me to lie there, helpless and spent on the cold, hard, dungeon floor.

3

Orion

"Am I doing this correctly?" the smith asked, wiping his brow. The lump of starsteel on the anvil glowed with heat from the forge, but despite his attempts to hammer it into shape, it refused to flatten.

"Not quite."

Using the tongs, I returned the lump of starsteel to the fire. But instead of simply shoving it into the heart of the flames, I lowered it slowly, and only halfway down.

"See how the metal is beginning to soften?" I squished it with the tongs, demonstrating its newfound pliancy.

"Surely the temperature is too low to soften it so quickly!" he exclaimed.

"That is the secret to working with starsteel. It must be heated slowly, to a temperature that is lower than what it takes to smelt iron or regular steel," I explained.

"How strange," he murmured, watching carefully as I slowly withdrew the metal and placed it back on the anvil.

"Try shaping it now." I stood back as the smith took a few experimental swings at the metal. A grin broke out on his face when the metal flattened easily.

"What a finicky metal."

"Indeed. It will only harden if heated quickly to high temperatures." I watched raptly as the smith folded the starsteel, eliminating any impurities and strengthening it layer by layer.

Soon, the dagger began to take shape. But before he could plunge the finished blade into the cooling trough of water, I gestured for him to follow me outside. The night air was pleasantly cool against my flushed skin after the heat of the forge. Despite the thick canopy, I was still able to make out a handful of stars twinkling above us. I felt the now-familiar hum of my magic awakening at the starlight's touch, silvering my hair and eyes.

"Hold the metal up to the starlight," I instructed.

He did so, and gasped when the metal began to glow and shine in reaction. He turned it this way and that, marveling as the magic of the stars entered the starsteel, strengthening it and marking it with a constellation.

"Try touching it with your bare hand."

"I only fell for that trick once," the muscled druid grumbled.

"Trust me—you will not be burned."

The smith removed his thick glove and cautiously touched a finger to the flat of the blade. He scowled, then looked at me in confusion. "It is cold. Did you do this?"

I grinned. "All starsteel weapons and tools are finished in the starlight. It is how we imbue a kernel of starlight magic into them—the magic that cancels out all others."

"No wonder we could never replicate a blade from Astoria," he mumbled, looking in awe at the dagger.

A thought tickled the back of my mind. "If you have any, could I see what weapons you forged of starsteel before today?"

"Hm? Oh yes, of course." The druid smith led the way around to the back of the smithy, and opened the doors of what appeared to be an armory. "The failed starsteel experiments are in the back corner there."

I walked over to the corner he indicated. It was piled high with various starsteel tools and weapons that were largely malformed and lumpy. I could tell at a glance that although the smiths had occasionally lucked into heating the metal slowly, none had truly discerned the proper method.

I picked up a misshapen sword, inspecting it closely. It appeared that its creator had attempted to mix another metal into the starsteel, to make it more pliable. And although it did feel...off, it certainly did not cut me off from my magic with a simple touch, like the witch's corrupted starsteel had.

I examined a few more of the items, but none of them had that horrible effect. After the witches' attack, I had realized that once my people discovered the secret to forging starsteel, we had stopped innovating with it. Perhaps it was time to change that.

I returned to the forge, where the smith was lovingly wrapping the hilt of the dagger with leather strips for the grip.

"I would like to commission you for a particular project," I began.

The smith's eyes lit up, and he grinned with unabashed delight. "What did you have in mind?"

I blew out a shaky breath to calm the nervous excitement in the pit of my stomach as I walked through the gardens. I had been so engrossed in my discussion with the smith that I had lost track of time. I glanced up at the stars as I picked up the pace. What would my parents think of the alliances I had forged? Of the way I had been learning to wield the magic my mother had gifted me?

I spotted Queen Rowena where she waited for me, within a secluded grove in a corner of the palace's extensive gardens. Worry furrowed her brow as she gazed at a patch of moonflowers, and I could guess what caused it.

"Thank you for waiting, Your Majesty. Have you been here long?" I asked as I approached.

She gave me a wan smile. "I only just arrived."

"How did your dinner with Rafe go?" I asked tentatively. It had been awkward between them ever since the queen had recognized the wolf shifter as her long-lost son. Although he had been reluctant at first, Rafe had agreed to spend some time with her. Though he was clearly uncomfortable here, I was sure he would get used to it eventually.

"Better than the last one," she chuckled drily.

"I am glad to hear it. Did he remember to use a knife and fork this time?" I had heard from Ivy that even when in druid form, Rafe tended to behave as if he were still a wolf.

"Yes, thankfully. He *is* a quick learner. Then again, he always was...even when he was an infant," she trailed off, her eyes clouding with distant memories. Then she cleared her throat, her emerald eyes finding mine. "But enough about that. Let us begin your final lesson. Are you ready?"

I dipped my head. I had been both dreading and eagerly anticipating this moment since we had begun our nightly training sessions. During the day, I trained in the sword, and during the night, I learned how to wield my magic. It was easier at night, when the stars augmented the magic within me.

"Good. Now that you have learned how to reliably and consistently locate and call upon your magic, you will practice using it."

"How do druids use their magic without a conduit?" I asked. Before, I had only been able to grant wishes while I held my mother's star sapphire amulet. But I had never seen a druid use anything of the sort while wielding their wild magic.

"We connect the magic that dwells within us to the magic that is all around us, in every aspect of nature. What differentiates us from the witches is that they can only use the finite amount of magic contained within themselves. To cast larger, more permanent magics, they must steal the magic of other things. They, however, do not view magic and lifeforce as separate, which is why they commonly sacrifice plants and animals to cast their more malicious hexes."

I scowled. "Is that why all—or at least, most—witches appear so...aged, and haggard?"

"Yes. they often inadvertently use their own lifeforce, along with their magic, and that drains the vitality from their bodies. And although they perform rituals to steal and absorb the lifeforce of others to unnaturally extend their lives, that cannot undo the damage to their bodies," she explained.

"Which is why Adelaide still looks her age. She was not able to use her magic until recently." Her name felt bitter on my tongue.

"In contrast, we druids call upon the magic of nature, the magic in the earth, the water, and the sky. We do not touch any lifeforce; we use only nature's overflowing abundance of magic." The queen paused to meet my eyes. "Since fallen stars draw magic from both themselves and from the stars above, I believe the process should be similar for you."

"I certainly hope so," I muttered. Her eyes softened.

"Now, let us start small." The queen paused thoughtfully, and picked a single moonflower from the garden. She tore one of the petals and held it out to me. "I wish for this flower's petal to be made whole."

I took it carefully and closed my eyes, taking a deep breath to steady my nerves. This was the moment I had been practicing for. If I could learn this, then I might just be able to save Astrid—along with the rest of my people.

I followed the path in my mind I had memorized, reaching for the core within me where my magic dwelled. It stirred lazily, but then came alive when I called it forth. I guided it to my hands, though for a moment I struggled with keeping the flow of magic stable. I thought I had it, until it slipped away from my control.

I growled in frustration. When I opened my eyes, starlight glowed in the air around me, but the petal remained torn. I scowled. Was it really impossible for me to channel this vast amount of magic alone?

If I kept failing like this, I would never be able to save Astrid in time.

"Do not lose heart," the queen said as she set a comforting hand on my shoulder. "Few druids succeed the first time, either."

I nodded, took a breath, and tried again. And again. But the magic resisted my control. I had thought practicing at night would make this easier, but having so much power at my disposal was actually making it that much harder to wield.

"What am I doing wrong?" I ground my teeth in frustration.

"Talk me through the steps. Which part of the process is giving you trouble?" Queen Rowena asked.

"There is simply too much magic in the air." I ran a hand through my hair. "I cannot control it all and grant the wish at the same time."

"Hmm." She pursed her lips. "When you used the amulet, did you use the same amount of power to heal a scratch as you would to heal a mortal wound?"

"Of course not."

"So why are you trying to control so much magic at once? Can you not call upon only a sliver of starlight—just enough to mend this small tear?"

"Oh." I blinked. I had been trying to control all of it at once on instinct. But the queen was right—I only needed a tiny amount of magic to knit a flower petal back together. "Let me try again."

I closed my eyes, focusing on the magic. Instead of trying to bend all of it to my will, I tried a different strategy. I clenched my jaw, imagining a dam that allowed only a small amount of magic to leak through. I pulled at that thin thread of magic, and sealed the dam once more when I felt I had enough.

I felt the cool whisper of starlight as it pooled in my hands, and opened my eyes to see my skin glowing with silvery light. With that magic as an anchor, I practiced pulling a tad more starlight to my hands from the air around me, until wisps of it wreathed the moonflower in its glow. Now, I had the right amount of magic for this sort of wish.

Just as I had when I used the amulet, I visualized the moonflower's petal being knit back together. I guided the magic into the flower and willed it to fulfill the wish that had been spoken.

The flower glowed as brightly as its namesake, but I continued exerting my will over the magic until I saw that the petal had been so completely mended that I could not tell it had ever been torn.

A bright, burning pain flared in a single point on my back, and I grimaced. But then I broke into a huge grin. *I had done it!* For the first time, I had consciously, purposefully, granted a wish *without* relying on the amulet. I could hear the phantom sound of the door of possibility creaking open before me. Now, I could confidently grant wishes. And most importantly of all, now I could save Astrid from her curse!

"Are you in pain? Did something go wrong?" Queen Rowena asked worriedly, stepping forward.

I just shook my head and handed her the healed flower. "No, it went right. I was able to grant your wish, without relying on a conduit! There is just always some pain in my back whenever I grant another's wish."

She frowned. "Show me."

After only a moment of hesitation, I drew my tunic over my head and turned my back to the queen, baring the constellations inked across my skin to her.

She gasped as her eyes scanned the glowing stars on my back. The sting began to fade, but I could tell that a new star had appeared just under my left shoulder blade.

"Does a new star appear every time you grant a wish?"

"Yes."

She reached out a hand, and gently touched a point near the top of my spine. "This one has gone dark. Do you have any idea why?"

I thought back over the last month, and I suddenly realized that there had only been one time when the process had felt different. "Normally, I feel a sharp, burning pain when a new star is formed on my back. But the one and only time I made and granted my *own* wish, to heal my friend Rigel of his mortal wound, I felt that star turn to ice. But I had not realized that meant it went out."

"How curious," she murmured.

"What is?"

"Each star is a miniature store of starlight—of magic," she elaborated. "As far as I can tell, each one will remain sealed until a specific condition is met. What that condition is, however, I cannot say."

I frowned. "A condition, huh?" There had been too many variables that night for me to be certain which one, or which combination of factors, had allowed me to access one of these stores of magic. And I was not exactly keen on the idea of recreating such a nightmarish situation in order to find out.

"Did your mother also bear these constellations on her back?" The queen asked as I tugged my tunic back on.

I shook my head. "My father never mentioned anything of the sort."

"Perhaps this is a trait unique to a child of a human and a fallen star. I suppose there is no way to know for certain, unfortunately."

I sighed. "Unfortunately," I echoed. For the thousandth time, I wished I could have had the chance to know my mother. A familiar ache rose in my chest as I glanced up at the stars. There were so many questions I wanted to ask her.

"I am sure you will discover the answers in due time." She gave me a motherly smile that made a lump rise in my throat. "For now, please accept my congratulations on successfully granting your first wish, wholly unaided. I am expecting great things from you, Prince Sterling."

"Thank you for your guidance, Queen Rowena." I returned her smile. Her attitude towards me had thawed a great deal over the last few days.

"I will take my leave so you can get some rest. I will see you and the others off in the morning."

4

Orion

I tossed and turned, trying to get comfortable in the downy bed of one of the palace's guest rooms. But no matter what I did, my heart continued to race, and my mind refused to shut down. Excitement and dread chased each other around my stomach, and I could hardly keep my eyes closed. How could I, when a whole new world of possibility had just opened up before me?

With a heavy sigh, I gave up on trying to catch a wink of sleep tonight. I rose from the bed and paced over to the small balcony. A cool breeze whispered across my dampened skin as I leaned against the railing and gazed out over the quiet gardens. But as usual, my eyes and my thoughts were soon drawn upwards to the stars. It was easier to see them from the forest than from the castle back in Astoria, due to the lack of lampposts and torches here.

The stars glittered like gemstones on a bed of crushed velvet, but for some reason, they did not feel quite as cold or as distant as usual. I wondered if Astrid could see the stars from wherever she was being held. By the stars, I hoped she was safe. If only she were still here—I could have tried to grant her wish and dispel the curse that she had borne alone for far too long.

That way, she would not have to bind herself to this far-away forest forever.

I gripped the railing of the balcony, my knuckles turning white. The thought of losing Astrid—either to that infernal curse, or Nyra, or this forest, was driving me insane. But even if—no, *when*—I rescued her from the clutches of the tribesmen, what if she chose to return to the Druidlands? To the loving aunt she had finally reconnected with? With her grandfather gone, there was no reason for her not to assume her title and succeed her aunt as the next Druid Queen.

A muscle feathered in my jaw. I thought back to every stolen touch, every moonlit stroll and steamy kiss we had shared aboard the *StarSeeker*. Our voyage here had felt like a dream. And without her, I was living in a waking nightmare. I did not want to even think about what I would do if I found her too late, or if she chose to live in Sylvaine with her aunt.

I did not want to ascend the throne without her by my side. Why had it taken me so long to realize that?

I closed my eyes, and practiced finding and calling forth my own inner starlight. A hum of power filled my veins, and I could tell without looking that I was glowing. Now that I had a handle on my power, I vowed that I would not let it go to waste.

I snapped my eyes open. Instead of letting my worries consume me, perhaps I should practice putting this power to good use. The stars knew that would be a better use of my time than letting my worries consume me.

My mind made up, I quietly dressed, strapped on my starsword, and exited my room as silently as I could. I closed the door softly, not wanting to disturb anyone else at this late hour.

"Trouble sleeping?"

I whirled, my hand finding the hilt of my sword. Noctus was leaning against the wall in a pocket of shadow, where neither the moonlight nor the glowing moss lanterns could reach. With an exasperated sigh, I let my hand fall to my side.

"How did you know?" I grumbled as I began walking down the hall.

Noctus chuckled, as he pushed off the wall to follow. "Because I know *you.*"

"It seems you know me better than I do."

"I wonder," came the quiet reply. "So, what will it be tonight? Stargazing? Sparring?"

I shook my head. He really did know me that well, faithful shadow that he was. "Wish granting."

The sound of Noctus' steps faltered, and then he ran up and clapped me on the back in a rare show of affection. "Congratulations! I knew you would figure it out in no time."

"Thank you." I smiled. "Since there is no way I can fall asleep, I decided I may as well get some more practice in before we leave."

"In that case, you may be interested to know that I just so happen to know of a number of druids in need of some wish granting. Starting with those still in the infirmary." Noctus smirked at me knowingly.

I laughed. "Lead the way."

The rest of the night passed in a blur of starlight and tears of pain and gratitude. I was able to heal most of the more grievously injured druids, whose wounds even druid magic had struggled to fully mend. I even came across a handful of cases where a witch's hex had lingered.

At first, I feared I would be unable to dispel the foreign, malicious magic without the amulet. Noctus suggested the victims hold onto my starsword to help dispel the effects. I readily agreed, and was thrilled when I was able to grant that druid's wish to be made whole without straining myself.

I relished the burning sensation in my back every time I successfully granted another wish. It was a heady sensation, to be able to help these people with my *own* power, without relying on an amulet or anything else to help me.

As the hours dragged on, the well of magic within me began to run dry. Fortunately, I had enough juice to heal everything beyond what druid magic could easily fix. And I was glad to have learned how deep the well of my magic ran, so that I would know when to stop in the future.

The joyful faces and heartfelt thanks of those I had helped and their loved ones reminded me why I had started my guild, Hyperion, in the first place. It was for moments like these, where love and relief and gratitude were so thick in the air that it felt like a warm embrace. A steady sense of determination welled up in my core with a force to rival my starlight.

I would save Astrid.

I would retake Astoria.

And once I did, I would bring joy and peace with me.

"It is nearly dawn. We need to prepare to leave," Noctus reminded me.

I glanced out a window, surprised to see that the sky was beginning to lighten. With a nod, I led the way out of the infirmary, and smiled to myself when a chorus of thank-yous and well-wishes rang out behind me.

"Please, Prince Sterling. Allow me to come with you." Rafe stood barring the way into my room. His arms were crossed, and he looked like he was ready for a fight. His short, blonde hair stuck up in odd places, as if he had not slept either. Though he now looked more like a druid, with pointed ears and all, he still did not act like one.

I narrowed my eyes. "Your place is here."

"My place is with Adelaide." He must have seen the rage in my eyes at her name, so he hurried to add, "I know what you must be thinking, and I do not blame you. But she is a good person at heart—she is just confused right now."

"Confused?" Noctus scoffed.

"You shielded her with your body, and she left you to die amongst the enemy she had just betrayed." Just the memory of that day made me burn with righteous indignation.

Rafe flinched, but his golden eyes did not waver. "They abused her for her entire life. The Headwitch has brainwashed her into believing that by capturing you, her powers will be fully unsealed as a reward, and she will reclaim her honor and her place in the coven."

I paused, but then shook my head, refusing to feel an ounce of pity or sympathy for the treacherous witch. "That is no excuse for what she has done. If she stands between me and Astrid again, I will not hesitate to cut her down."

Rafe paled a bit, and clenched his hands into fists. Noctus stiffened, readying himself to defend me from the wolf shifter.

He loosened his fists, and his eyes took on a desperate light. "I love her. I love her the way you love Astrid."

I stilled.

Rafe continued, "Let me come with you so that I can try to talk some sense into her. She will listen to me."

"And if she does not?"

"She will."

There was not a shred of doubt in his golden eyes. Rafe had absolute faith in her, even after what had happened.

I sighed. "You entered the druid's Sacred Heart, their source of magic. Are you not bound to this forest, the way your mother is?"

He half-closed his eyes for a moment, as if he were searching internally. "I am not. Not fully. I can leave for a time, but will have to return eventually. The witch magic in me made the binding looser." Noctus glanced at me.

I crossed my arms over my chest. If he could somehow get Adelaide to stand down, or even help us, I would be foolish to refuse. But would I be a fool to trust him? I supposed at the very least, he could distract Adelaide while we rescued Astrid.

"If you endanger this mission or harm myself or anyone else other than a tribesperson…" I let the threat hang in the air, but to the shifter's credit, he nodded in solemn acceptance. "Then you had better go pack. We leave at dawn."

The rising sun tinged the sky a stunning shade of tangerine, though a good portion of the sight was blocked by the small fleet of starships that hovered just above Pyrcairn. Their imposing silhouettes sent a shiver down my spine that had nothing to do with the chill in the air.

Queen Rowena stood regally before me, in the large courtyard in front of the palace, flanked by the Queen's Riders. Ivy winked at me when I spotted her standing proudly amongst them. It would seem she had been promoted after her contributions during the battle with the witches. I was happy for her.

Raiden and Birken each stood at the head of a sizable squadron of druid warriors. They would be boarding the starships with Noctus, Rafe and me, as our reinforcements for the mission to retake the castle. I had been surprised to learn that they had both volunteered to join. Raiden's reasoning I understood; he believed me to be the starborn prince of prophecy. But I had been under the impression that Birken held no such convictions.

"I speak on behalf of my people when I wish you good fortune in battle, and starspeed in reaching our long-lost Princess Elowen. The Woman-King shall regret making an enemy of Sylvaine!" Despite her drawn expression, the queen's voice rang out with steely determination and regal authority.

The druids roared their approval, startling the birds into flight. They stamped their spears into the ground in unison, the sound echoing loudly through the forest.

"As the rightful Prince of Astoria, I thank you for your support, and for your bravery. Our common foe, the tribesmen, who have blatantly trespassed in both our lands and kidnapped

Princess Elowen, will now face the consequences of their acts of aggression and treachery!" I declared.

My words were met with cheers as well. For the first time since Nyra had betrayed me, I felt like a prince, instead of a fugitive. And as the lifeboats descended to ferry the druids up to the fleet of starships, I noticed the queen's gaze kept straying to Rafe. I nudged him forward, and did my best not to eavesdrop as they said their rather awkward goodbyes.

Once he returned to his place behind me, I stepped forward to speak with the queen. "Thank you for allowing our fleet to hover above Pyrcairn under these...unusual circumstances. I know this would normally be forbidden."

"Thank you for what you did last night in the infirmary." There was a hint of gratitude and approval in her gemstone eyes that had once looked at me with distrust.

"It was the right thing to do. And I welcomed the additional practice," I said with a small smile.

"I may have judged you too quickly," she murmured, her gaze finding the last load of druid warriors as they were ferried aboard a starship. "Please send as many back to me as you can."

My eyes widened a fraction. That was as close to an apology as I was likely to receive from her. "I will do my utmost—as your ally, and as the Starborn Prince."

Queen Rowena went still, before her eyes cut to Raiden. "I see you have spoken with Raiden."

I inclined my head.

"I never put much faith in the ramblings of an old druid when I was a youngling." Her eyes slid back to me.

"And now?"

"Now, I am learning to keep an open mind." Her gaze alighted on Rafe for a moment before it returned to me. "Life has a way of unfolding in unexpected and amazing ways. Perhaps you will surprise me yet."

"Whatever the stars have in store, I hope to surprise you for many years to come—alongside Astrid."

I nodded my head to her respectfully and stepped into the lifeboat, smiling to myself at the knowing look on her face. It was a roundabout way of declaring my intentions, but we no longer had the luxury of time and formalities.

As Noctus, Rafe and I rose towards the open sky, and the fleet of starships that awaited us, I took out my starsteel watch and sent a starnote to Rigel. It read:

Prepare to overthrow the Woman-King.

5

Astrid

"Your feast has arrived, *Your Highness,*" Helga sneered through the bars of the cell. She held a small wooden tray in her gnarled hands.

I had not seen Adelaide for several days. Instead, this other witch had been bringing me old leftovers and calling them meals.

She shoved the piece of stale bread and the bowl of thin soup through the narrow slot at the bottom of the door in such a way that half the broth sloshed out onto the dirty stone floor.

"Your eyes must be as useless as your nose." I wrinkled my own nose at the little tray, despite the ache of hunger in my belly. There was no point in even trying to eat that muck: I would only throw it up when the next curse-induced seizure hit.

"How *dare* you speak to me that way!" Helga snarled. She curled her knobby hands into fists at her side.

I raised an eyebrow at her. "What are you going to do—kill me?"

Helga's face was turning an alarming shade of red, and a vein stood out on her wrinkled forehead. It was strange to think that we were not so far apart in age, especially considering that she looked old enough to be my grandmother.

"You and that stupid, powerless witch Adelaide need to learn your place!" Helga seethed. Wisps of discordant magic began to swirl around her.

"Feel free to let me out then, so that I can do that." I wrapped my arms around my knees, which I had pulled close to my chest for warmth. "Oh wait, I forgot. Your Headwitch would never trust you with the keys."

I turned my head away dismissively, and watched from the corner of my eye as Helga's face turned from red to a mottled purple. Adelaide had known me well enough to wise up to my goading, but this witch... This witch was easy to manipulate.

"Headwitch Brunhilde is the most powerful witch to have led the Redgraves in generations—and *I* will be the one to succeed her!" Helga scowled as she fished out an iron key, and brandished it towards me smugly. "Of course she trusts me with the key."

I pretended to gasp, and schooled my expression into one of surprise and fear. When Helga inserted the key into the lock, I hid my elation that my plan was working. Instead, I jumped to my feet and shuffled nervously towards the back of my cell.

"Too late to act all meek now," Helga purred as the iron door swung open and she slowly advanced, clearly reveling in my feigned terror.

"Wait, stop! Do not come any closer," I stammered, cowering away from the witch and her malevolent magic, while slowly reaching for the weapon I had concealed in my skirts.

Once Helga had begun delivering my meals, I had been quick to notice her carelessness. And if *I* had noticed, everyone else would have as well. So when she came to collect my empty soup bowl a few days ago, she had never even noticed the spoon was missing. The kitchen staff likely would have assumed the witch had dropped it, and been too afraid to ask after it. It had taken longer than I anticipated to sharpen the end of the spoon by scraping it against the rough stone floor, but I had done it.

Now, I had no illusions that I could take out a witch with a sharpened spoon. But perhaps if I aimed for her eye...then I could attempt to make a run for it.

"Too little, too late. I am going to make you regret ever talking back to me." Helga smiled cruelly as brown magic the color of dried blood rapidly gathered around her raised hands.

My heart pounded in my ears, and I had to remind myself to breathe. This particular trick would only work *once*. I had to get this right.

"That is *my* line." In one fluid motion, I stood up straight, drew my mini stake, pulled my arm back, and drove it towards her yellowed eye with all the strength I could muster.

The tip of my improvised stake slammed to a stop, mere inches from Helga's eye, as if it had hit an invisible wall. I scowled, confused. Based on the look of utter shock and fear on Helga's face, this shield was not her doing.

I tried to dart around Helga, hoping to still salvage my plan. And...ran straight into the invisible shield. I felt along it with my hands, looking for an opening, but it extended across the entirety of my cell.

Helga fell back on her bony rear. If this was not her doing, then... I glared at the shadows where the dim torchlight failed to reach.

"Quit hiding and show yourself, traitor," I hissed, trying to redirect my frustration and helplessness into anger.

Adelaide strode forward, startling Helga, who quickly scrambled to her feet and out of my cell, before quickly locking it with shaking hands.

"The weak learn to become crafty. You would do well to remember that, Helga," Adelaide said to Helga with quiet venom. I sensed there was a double meaning to her words, that she was talking about more than just my failed attempt at escape.

Helga sputtered indignantly, then scoffed as a bit of color returned to her face. "Perhaps I should just punish the druid halfling from afar."

"We need her *alive* to be effective bait," Adelaide pointed out.

"But how would the starborn spawn know whether she was alive or not?" Helga smiled smugly.

"What if he still has spies within these walls? Do you really want to be the reason the Redgraves fail to capture him? We both know what fate awaits those who fail *this* particular mission." Adelaide's voice held a note of bitterness I was not expecting, but despite that, I could see that her hands were trembling.

Helga scoffed. "As if *I* would ever make the same mistake as your failure of a mother."

Had Adelaide's mother been tasked with capturing Orion's mother? Based on how they were speaking, it did not sound as if such a failure had been taken well. Knowing how cruel witches were to others, I shuddered to think how they tortured each other.

Adelaide scowled, but made no reply, and a cruel smirk twisted Helga's thin lips. Seeing Adelaide's reaction seemed to settle Helga's nerves, and she puffed out her chest and put a little more sass into her shuffling steps.

"That halfling is not the only one who needs to be taught a lesson," Helga said as she approached Adelaide, like a predator stalking its prey.

Adelaide took a step back, and then another, retreating from the other witch. She lowered her eyes submissively, adopting the same posture I had seen her use when her headwitch was present. Before my eyes, she practically transformed from a knowledgeable and crafty young woman to a cowering and fearful victim.

That same, awful-looking magic began to gather around Helga once more. She was clearly preparing to hex Adelaide. But instead of gathering her own magic, Adelaide just stood there, as if she had been expecting this. As if she were used to it.

"Tell that snake Nyra that I will be expecting some actual food to be brought to me," I ordered loudly.

As expected, Helga whirled, her eyes blazing with anger at my tone, and lashed out with her magic. I flinched, but her hex hit the shield in my cell and evaporated in a puff of smoke.

"How *dare* you order *me*— "

I picked up my sharpened spoon and held it to my throat, and Helga froze. "Shall we test how quickly a starnote can reach Prince Sterling?"

Helga looked dumbfounded, and I could practically hear her grinding her teeth. She abruptly turned and stormed towards the exit, calling over her shoulder, "Get that stupid spoon away from her and clean up this mess."

We both stood staring at each other long after the clang of the dungeon's heavy door stopped echoing through the stone halls. I did not thank Adelaide, and she did not thank me.

As the adrenaline wore off, however, I stumbled back to the stone wall of my cell, and slowly slid back to the cold floor. I let the sharpened spoon clatter onto the stone, and watched, too exhausted to move, as Adelaide floated the little piece of wood between the bars and into her waiting hand. With a wave of her hand, the spilled broth vanished, and the little tray moved slowly over to me, as if pushed by an invisible hand.

I stared at it as I listened to her stand there, staring at me for a minute. I said nothing. But as she walked away, I whispered, "If *that* is how they treat you, why would you ever want to earn a place among them?"

Adelaide paused. "The Redgraves are my family. My home. I have never known any different."

I slowly turned my head to look at her. "We both know that is not true."

Uncertainty and pain flickered in her red eyes for a moment before she turned away. Without another word, she left, her hand still tightly clutching my improvised weapon.

6

Orion

I ducked as a wooden practice sword whistled over my head, then jumped to the left and back to avoid two more attacks. I raised my heavy wooden shield to intercept the next blow, and thrust my own practice sword at the soldier's chest before he could recover. My opponent crouched down to catch his breath and signal that he had been "killed."

"Better," Leo grunted as I skipped backwards to give myself some breathing room. He oversaw this little exercise from his spot by the mainmast, with his arms crossed over his chest.

I nodded, too out-of-breath to respond. Five Harlandish soldiers and three of Jolene's crew still stood, though I had defeated one soldier and two crewmates already. I used the brief reprieve to catch my breath. We had been using wooden swords and shields that weighed double what our own weapons did, thanks to the lead pellets distributed evenly within the wood. My muscles ached, and my arms trembled from the strain, but I reveled in the discomfort.

This would be nothing compared to what was coming.

Every day since we had left the Druidlands, I had been training for the battle that awaited us in Astoria. Since I anticipated being faced with a solo battle against a group of tribesmen again, I had begun holding these training sessions with groups of my newfound allies. I glanced across the deck to see Noctus and Rafe doing the same; they were each surrounded by their own group of druids and soldiers.

I raised the tip of my sword, which I had allowed to droop, as two soldiers charged in close. I parried one blow and dodged the second, sneaking in a blow of my own before the second could recover. I cursed under my breath when the blade merely glanced off of his arm. Only by hitting a vital point could I "defeat" my opponents.

After all, Nyra had my mother's amulet, and she was not afraid to use it. At least *this* time, she would not be the *only* one capable of healing wounded allies.

My wandering thoughts cost me, and I hissed as a wooden blade scraped against my arm. I twisted to the side to avoid the follow-up strike, and slammed my shield into him and quickly tapped him on the neck before he could recover his balance.

"Keep your focus, Orion," Leo warned, as three more took the fallen's place. "Even a scratch can be deadly."

I gritted my teeth, the memory of Nyra's poisoned blade sobering me instantly. Even if I were surrounded, I needed to be able to avoid even the smallest scratch from a tribesman's scimitar. Perhaps I could cobble together some make-shift leather armor and chainmail for myself and my allies to prevent such an eventuality.

This time, I went on the offensive, calling on my years of training with the royal guards, and adding in some of the tricks Jolene had taught me on the way here. I jabbed one soldier in the chest and whirled unexpectedly towards one of Jolene's crew. Taking her by surprise, I slipped my sword around her guard and tapped her lightly on the throat.

I jumped over the sword that whistled through the air where my legs had just been, and I used my added height and momentum to bring a crushing vertical blow down on that soldier's head. He stumbled back, stunned, and I found myself grinning as I faced down the rest of my opponents all at once.

My heart was pounding in my chest and my breath came in ragged gasps, but I found I had entered that special state of mind where I could concentrate for hours without noticing the passage of time. This consistent practice had boosted my experience with fighting large groups at once, and therefore my confidence had risen as well. Instead of feeling afraid or nervous, I felt excited. I felt invincible.

I flourished my dull wooden blade and charged forward with a grin, imagining every strike of my blade felling one of the tribesmen standing between me and Astrid.

I lifted the hem of my tunic to wipe the sweat from my brow with hands that trembled from exhaustion. After my initial bout of group combat, I had switched to individual sparring sessions with Jolene, Leo, Raiden, Noctus and Regis. I had paid extra attention to each individual's unique fighting style, as I was determined to incorporate their moves into my own style of combat.

I had a feeling I was going to need every trick and tactic I could find to beat Nyra and her warriors once and for all.

I felt a hint of magic tingle across my skin, so I pulled out my starsteel watch and walked into the shadow cast by the mainmast, so I could more easily read the glowing letters. I felt more than saw Noctus join me, but he waited patiently for me to read the message first.

"According to Rigel, things have taken a turn for the worse." I frowned.

"How so?"

"Nyra has completely stopped granting any wishes at all—even those of her own people."

Now it was Noctus' turn to scowl. "She had no problem using the amulet before. Why has that changed?"

"Could she be trying to store up its power to attempt to grant a difficult wish? Will she finally try to restore the oases in the Tribelands?"

"She would be foolish to disregard your warnings and attempt it herself, with only that amulet," Noctus mused.

I narrowed my eyes as I met his gaze. "What if she drained its magic completely? And has yet to figure out how to recharge it?"

"Hmm. That could be..." Noctus tilted his head. "But surely the amulet would have reached its limit weeks ago if that were the case, considering how many wishes she granted right after she...right after she took over."

"True." I crossed my arms over my chest, pushing aside the bloody memories his words conjured. "Unless she has just been pouring the liquid starlight reserves into it. We kept a sizable store on hand for emergencies." I hated to think that our huge stockpile had been wasted on granting the wishes of the usurpers.

"That would also explain why she forced the starships to sell all of their stock to her."

I nodded. "Both could be true. If my assistant Zale were clever enough to avoid imprisonment, he might be able to find out for us."

"Did Rigel say anything else?" Noctus prompted.

I looked down to continue reading. "Tribesmen have been forcibly taking over the homes of Astorians."

"Which means there is no longer enough room to hold them all in the castle," Noctus said grimly.

I grimaced. "Good thing we are not returning alone."

"How are the Astorians taking it?"

"Not well. It sounds like anger and resentment have begun to replace the people's fear. On the bright side, that means Rigel has been having an easier time recruiting more Astorians to our side." Which would hopefully help our plan go more smoothly.

"Took them long enough," Noctus grumbled.

I had to smile at that. "Rigel said he has sheltered a number of rebellious Astorians who were a tad too vocal about their...dissatisfaction, and had the misfortune of catching Nyra's attention. Though he also reports that a fair number have fled to neighboring towns, where her influence has yet to spread."

"Cowards."

"I once said the same, but...I understand their reasoning. Most are only looking to protect their families." I wondered fleetingly how Sirius, Estelle, Celeste, Nova and Castor were doing. I hoped they were safe and relaxed in the little house by the lake.

Noctus' gaze softened. "Fleeing now will do them little good if that means Astoria remains in Nyra's clutches. Her reach may not extend past the capitol *now*, but it *will* eventually, if left unchecked."

"Fear can make people short-sighted," I agreed. "At least that means Rigel is having little difficulty preparing housing for our new allies."

Noctus simply nodded.

"I will update Rigel on our status, and the number of beds we will be needing. And I will see if he has been able to get in contact with Zale. While I do, could you fetch Jolene?"

Noctus returned with Jolene just as I sent the starnote. I updated her on what we had learned from Rigel, and she had a few suggestions for me of which starship captains might be swayed to our cause, which I then promptly relayed to Rigel.

"Anything else you needed to discuss with me?" she asked.

"Could I commission you and the other captains to ferry those who wish to flee to safety before we attack?" I wanted to minimize casualties as much as I could, since Nyra surely would not.

"Some may be willing to carry passengers away, but I cannot guarantee all of them will return for more," she said grimly.

"So long as we still have enough starships for our forces, that is fine by me." We would be in trouble, though, if we found ourselves without any air support at all.

"That much, I can promise." Jolene nodded sternly. "You will have your ships, even if I have to commandeer them myself."

7

Orion

T he steady wind blew my glowing silver hair back from my damp forehead, but I could hardly feel the chill. I was too focused on the task at hand, since every time my concentration lapsed, I had to start over from scratch.

I continued to carefully guide the thin stream of liquid starlight out of the dark sky and into the glass bottle I held. Normally, collecting liquid starlight or processing stardust into its liquid form was a slow and arduous process, but after some trial and error, I was slowly learning how to do it myself using magic.

Initially, I had come up on deck just to gaze at the stars, since sleep eluded me. But after thinking about the depleted supply in the castle, I had wondered if there was a way for me to begin creating my own emergency supply—since I had a feeling I would be needing it.

The thought of executing the plan I had been hammering out with the others sent a shiver of nervous anticipation through me, and I sighed when the stream of starlight fizzled out. I refocused, and soon had a ribbon of silvery light dancing in front of me once more.

The stars glimmered in the distance, and an ache of loneliness pierced my heart. The last time I had been stargazing on the *StarSeeker*, Astrid had been right by my side. We had talked and laughed and danced under the moonlight, and I had finally mustered up the courage to kiss her.

Nothing was the same without her. Everything looked pale and lifeless, just as it had after Nyra had killed my father. Astrid had been the one who breathed light and hope into my life—so why had it taken me so long to realize it?

I grimaced as I recalled the look on Aria's face when I had returned without Astrid. She had yelled at me furiously, but I could see the sheen of tears in her eyes. Clearly, I was not the only one who felt her absence. I had promised I would save Astrid, but when the girl pointed out I had already promised to keep her safe, I had had nothing to say. She was right—I had failed Astrid. And Aria had been sullenly glaring at me ever since.

I could hardly blame her. But despite how upset she was with me, she had still insisted on helping get Astrid back. Knowing how stubborn she was, she would likely stow away with the soldiers if I told her to stay where it was safe. I would have to find a way to involve her that was not terribly dangerous.

But although I had already worked out plans A, B, and C, we were still a fair distance from Astoria. The trip to the Druidlands had gone by in a flash, but this return trip was crawling by at the pace of an exhausted snail. I had no idea how quickly Astrid's curse was eating away at her lifeforce, and the need to go to her was like an insatiable itch beneath my skin. While I was grateful for the chance to hone my swordsmanship and practice using my magic, I still wished we could move faster.

A muscle feathered in my jaw. I had already asked Raiden and Birken if they could use their magic to summon strong winds for us, but they could only do so for short intervals. That was not a magic they could keep up for weeks on end. Besides, it would pose a problem if they were both too exhausted to carry out the plan when we arrived.

A sudden gust buffeted me, as if it were mocking me. I stumbled, breaking the stream of starlight and causing a couple drops of liquid starlight to spill onto a rope at my feet.

I cursed my carelessness. But then I stared at the rope, which was slowly floating upwards. The sight made me recall an old story my father had told me, about how he and my mother had discovered that stardust could make things float. It appeared liquid starlight had a similar effect. An idea tickled the back of my mind, and I laughed aloud at my own foolishness.

"Have you gone mad?" Aria asked sleepily from behind me.

"Perhaps a little." I chuckled. "But what are you doing up?"

She rubbed at her eyes, but the starbird on her shoulder was too mesmerized by the floating rope and the bottle in my hand to protest being jostled. "Part of my duties are to make sure Arcturus collects enough stardust every night to make the ship float."

"A very important job." Aria still looked half-asleep, but what I said next perked her right up. "I think I know how we can get to Astrid faster."

She was wide-awake now. "How?!"

"Now that I have a better handle on my magic, what if I could grant a wish to make the starships move *faster?*"

Aria's eyes widened. "Would we no longer have to rely on the wind to move us?"

"Exactly!" I grinned. "But I am going to need your help. What do you say?"

"Absolutely! What do you need me to do?"

"I need you to make a wish—but you must word it precisely how I tell you. Can you do that for me?" This sort of wish would likely take a good amount of magic to grant, so I wanted to make sure we got it right the first time. That way, I would not have to wait for my magic to replenish before trying again.

"Yes—whatever you need." She set her chin, and I could tell she was determined.

I smiled, and proceeded to coach her on exactly what to say. She had a couple of suggestions, and since she had spent more time on starships than me, I decided to include them. After she could recite it flawlessly, I tapped into my well of magic and gave her a nod.

"I wish that the *StarSeeker*, *Windsnap*, *StarStream*, *SeaMaid*, and *SilverSail* could fly on their own, day and night, without the use of stardust, at four different speeds: floating, cruising, sailing, and racing. The captain and those the captain designates need only say float, cruise, sail, or race for the ship to move accordingly, and may adjust altitude by saying either lower, higher, or steady."

"Well done," I murmured as I closed my eyes.

My whole body buzzed with magic, and I carefully began channeling it to each of the five ships in our fleet. To my surprise, the stardust coating their hulls, plus the abundant starlight in the air, came alive to do my bidding. It tried to get away from me once or twice, to run wild in the night, but I held it in a firm mental grip, commanding it to alter the properties of each ship in order to grant the wish. To accomplish that, I tied in the potential for the magic to be strengthened and renewed when exposed to starlight, just to be safe.

As I released my hold on the magic, I felt the formation of a new star among the many constellations inked across my back. Despite the accompanying pain, I was grateful for the sensation, since I could be sure, without a doubt, that the wish had been fully granted.

I opened my eyes to a magnificent sight. The other starships in our fleet glowed silver in the moonlight, and each one left a trail of glimmering starlight in its wake.

"It feels as if we are riding a shooting star," Aria murmured in awe. The ships' glow was reflected in her wide eyes.

The starbird on her shoulder chirped, as if in agreement, before leaping from her shoulder and into the air. The proud creature was not one to be outdone, after all, and added his own faint trail of stardust to the sky as it cavorted along in our wake.

"It does make quite a sight." I smiled.

Aria glanced over at me, but then did a double take. "You are glowing even more than the ships!"

I looked down at myself in surprise, and raised my glowing hands in front of my face, turning them this way and that. Silvery light hovered on my skin like an ethereal mist, leaving trails behind whenever I moved. Miniature stars sparkled in the air around me, and I could feel my hair swishing through the air as if I were underwater.

"Well, this is new." This had definitely not happened when I granted wishes before. Did the scale of the wish or the amount of magic I used cause this? Or was it because this was the first wish I had granted so close to the stars?

Had my mother glowed like this when she fell to earth? When she granted wishes? How long would it last?

Aria sidled up to me and poked one of the little stars, which burst into a shower of smaller sparkles. They glowed for a moment when they landed on her, but that soon faded away as the starlight sank into her skin, causing her to glow for a few seconds as well.

She giggled, and circled around me, popping stars, until she was faintly glowing all over as well. I chuckled at her antics.

"Now, we just need to wake the captain and have her—"

The door to Captain Jolene's cabin slammed open, and she stumbled on deck in a comical state of undress. Tufts of her dark hair were sticking up in all directions, and she wore her nightclothes, the pants of which were stuffed into her leather boots. She looked around, bewildered, but her eyes soon settled on Aria and me.

"By the stars, what have you done to those ships? To *my* precious ship?!" She walked cautiously, as if the still-glowing wood beneath her feet was liable to snap at any moment.

"Orion granted my wish for the ships to move faster! I bet we will reach Astoria in half the time it normally takes!" Aria answered excitedly before I could get a word in.

"I would have liked to be consulted on this first, seeing as it is *my* ship you just magicked," Jolene grumbled, "How are we meant to ambush the enemy now? They will see us coming from miles away!" she protested.

I paused. I had not realized how brightly the ships might glow, and realized with a sinking feeling that I might have just blown our chances at an ambush. "I believe the glow should begin to fade soon. Even if it does not, I can either grant another wish to eliminate the glow, or we can ask the druids to give us some thick cloud cover when we get close."

"Or we could arrive during the day, one at a time, and sneak in with the other starships on Lake Hesperia," Aria suggested. "We can raise the Woman-King's flag to fool her tribesmen!"

"Good thing I had not gotten around to burning that rag just yet," the captain muttered, but then she smiled at Aria. "What good suggestions from my newest crewmate."

"Yes, excellent solution, Aria," I quickly added. Aria beamed at me, but Jolene raised an eyebrow.

I grinned sheepishly. Perhaps I should have thought this one through a little more first. "My apologies for doing this without your consent. I promise to ask you first in the future."

"You had better," she grumbled, but I could tell she was eyeing the sails with renewed interest. "Exactly how much faster are we talking here?"

I grinned, and proceeded to explain how the magic worked, and the commands that only the captain could give their ship. "Care to try it out for yourself?"

"I suppose." Captain Jolene walked to the helm, but despite her outward calm, I could tell by the set of her shoulders and the look in her emerald eyes that she was excited.

"*StarSeeker*, race!" she commanded the ship.

For a moment, nothing happened. But then, I felt the magic respond, and the starship lurched forward. It quickly picked up speed, until the wind on deck was so strong that it whipped our hair into our faces and caused the crewmembers on duty to scramble to trim the sails.

But Captain Jolene was grinning from ear to ear.

"Neither friend nor foe will be able to catch us now!" she shouted over the roar of the wind. "At this speed, we will reach Astoria in a matter of days!"

8

Astrid

I clenched my jaw as another uncontrollable spasm wracked my weakened body. Waves of agony radiated from my center as the curse consumed more and more of what little magic remained in me. The pain was nearly unbearable, which meant it had either begun eating away at my lifeforce, or it would very soon.

I resisted the urge to scream, knowing all it would get me was a beating from the dungeon guards, or more abuse from Helga. It had been several days since the confrontation between her and Adelaide, and I had not seen either one of the witches since. Now a scullery maid from the kitchens brought me my daily meal, which had gotten neither better nor worse.

My meal and the regular changing of the guards were my only indication that time was passing at all. With only a handful of torches for light, my sense of time had all but evaporated. Since my isolated cell was near the entrance to the dungeons, I had no way of learning who else Nyra had thrown down here. I was certain there were many, but I had no way to try to communicate with those who were imprisoned deeper inside.

There was nothing at all to do down here, besides eat, worry, and try to grit my teeth and bear the increasingly frequent seizures. I squeezed my eyes shut as another tremor went through me, then another, and another.

A groan slipped past my lips, and I curled up in a ball. I wished my pretty, useless dress provided some cushioning or warmth to ward off the damp chill that seemed more unbearable every night.

My hands trembled, and I struggled to stay conscious as the worst wave of pain yet sent icy fire through my veins. I feared that if I fell asleep, I would never wake again.

But the comforting nothingness of sleep beckoned me, licking at the edges of my mind.

Just as I was about to give in, I felt rough hands shaking my shoulders, and a far-away noise that could have been my name filtered through the haze of pain. A dusting of something warm and comforting was sprinkled on my skin, chasing away some of the pounding in my head.

Stardust? Was that Orion? My heart lifted, and I struggled to open my eyes, to say something. Had he come to take me home?

Powdery stardust touched my lips, and I managed to unclench my jaw just enough for some to be poured into my mouth. I swallowed some down, nearly choking, but the relief was almost instant.

Every muscle relaxed, and I could finally take a deep breath. I blinked my eyes open, but when the dim dungeon swam into focus, it was Adelaide who was hovering over me worriedly. She was kneeling on the stone floor beside me, cradling my head in one hand and holding my confiscated pouch of stardust in the other. I stared at her in confusion.

"I have little doubt I am not who you were hoping to see," she said wryly, correctly interpreting my expression.

"Why—" I coughed, my dry throat catching on the word. Adelaide helped me drink some cool, fresh water from her canteen, and I tried again. "Why are you helping me?"

"I... I do not know." Adelaide looked down, her brows pinching together.

I raised an eyebrow. Was this some sort of new ploy to regain my trust? Or was this simply her way of ensuring that the bait did not expire before I lured Orion to his own demise?

"I know what you are thinking—I am under no one's orders to do this for you." Adelaide bit her lip. "Headwitch Brunhilde and Helga would actually punish me if they knew."

"Then why take the risk?"

A range of emotions flitted across the witch's features, but she did not reply immediately. Did Adelaide truly not know the reason herself? Was she helping me on a whim? Or was there some part of her that felt guilty for her betrayal?

"Why did you defend me? On the ship?" she asked abruptly, without answering my question.

I blinked. "Because I trusted you."

"How could you possibly trust me, even after Jolene exposed my secret to everyone?" The witch looked utterly bewildered, as if she could not comprehend my reasoning.

"I already knew you were a witch."

Adelaide's red eyes widened in shock. "What? How... How did you figure it out? And *when* did you figure it out?"

"I knew from the day we first met," I answered truthfully. "When you shook my hand, you did not notice that I was wearing a starsteel ring."

Her hand flew to her eyes. "My glamour flickered."

"Yes."

She scowled. "Why did you never say anything? If you knew the truth, why would you risk bringing me back to Hyperion?"

"Regardless of what you were or where you came from, you still deserved the chance to make a new life for yourself. Your origins did not matter to any of us. They never did."

Adelaide just stared.

"I also felt empathy for you—even more so when you said you had been cast out of your homeland," I continued, and I saw a hint of understanding begin to dawn in her crimson eyes. "I saw myself in you. Being chased out of your people's lands, your powers sealed, and facing difficulties when you found yourself alone in a strange land...I know how that feels. We were both hurt and abandoned by the ones who were supposed to love and protect us."

Adelaide looked down. "I never expected anyone else could ever understand what it was like to be an outcast. At first, I thought you were all soft-hearted fools." She laughed, a broken sort of sound.

Despite myself, I smiled sadly as happy memories of time spent with my guildmates surfaced in my mind. "That description is not wholly inaccurate."

"But then, I realized I almost envied you. I thought you and the others were undeserving of such easy lives."

I snorted. My life had been anything *but* easy.

"It was only after I spent more time with you and the others, and learned about all of the challenges you have faced, that my envy changed into a sense of...awe."

"From what I have seen, such emotions are not common among witches," I commented. I watched the other girl's face closely, noting the hint of shame at my words. Her short time with us had not been enough to dislodge years of the witches' teachings.

"No. A true witch strikes terror into the weak hearts of her enemies, and fear and respect into the cores of her allies," Adelaide recited. But her voice was uncertain, as if she were questioning the wisdom of that adage.

"That sounds like a lonely existence." Perhaps it was foolish of me to comfort my captor. But I was enjoying my moments of painlessness, and a small part of me still wanted to reach the girl who had talked herbs with me until late into the night. If my words from before had reached her guilty conscience, then talking may lead to something good. I decided to take a gamble. "Rafe did not fear you."

Adelaide stiffened when I mentioned his name, but after another moment, she relaxed. "He never did." Her shoulders slumped, and silver lined her downcast red eyes.

It was the most emotion I had ever seen her show. It hit me, then. This black-hearted witch loved him. And she believed he was dead.

I bit my lip, remembering the way Rafe had yelped as he was knocked into the Sacred Heart's magic. Should I tell her what I had seen? But what if I was wrong? The smoke had partially obscured my vision, and even *I* was not entirely sure what I had witnessed was even possible.

"We do not know for sure that he..." I trailed off, testing the waters.

"Do not give me false hope," the witch snapped angrily, but I could see the way her lower lip trembled.

I placed a weak hand on her arm.

Adelaide met my eyes, conflict clear in the crimson depths. "Why are you trying to comfort me? I... I betrayed you!"

"I believe in judging people based on their actions, not their words." I smiled sadly and bit my tongue, refusing to give voice to the additional thought that I had regretted doing just that. I sensed a change in Adelaide, and did not want my lingering resentment to interfere with that. "That is why I shared my home and my family with you and Rafe. Everyone deserves a second chance. Even those who have wronged us."

The tears that had been gathering in her eyes spilled over, flowing down her cheeks like a silver stream. "How can you say that? How can you be so disgustingly kind?"

My laugh quickly turned into a cough, and Adelaide rubbed my back soothingly. Despite her upbringing, the witch was kinder than even she wanted to admit.

"Because..." I trailed off as my gaze lifted to the stone ceiling, my mind imagining all the stars I could not see. "Because that is something Orion would have done. And he has always inspired me to be a better person."

A tear traced a cool line down my cheek at the thought that I was never going to see him again. I was too weak to try and escape again. "And because I love him so, I am still trying to be a better person—even if I know I will never get to see him again." I turned my eyes back to Adelaide, and lifted my hand to her cheek. "Just like the way you tried to be better for Rafe, Adele."

The witch held me close, her silent sobs wracking her thin frame. We held each other as we cried, a witch and a druid united in our love for those we would never meet again.

9

Orion

I had never seen a more beautiful or bittersweet sight. My home, my kingdom lay spread out below me, gilded by the setting sun. The silhouettes of Astor Castle's spear-like towers scraped the sky, and I wanted nothing more than to burn the cursed flags that now flew from their spires.

But more than anything, I desperately hoped Astrid was still hanging in there. I had little doubt as to how Nyra was treating her. The moment she was within my sight, I intended to make and grant a wish to save her from her grandfather's curse.

And if that traitorous witch Adelaide dared to get in my way... Rafe might not be able to hold me back.

"Quite the sight for sore eyes," Noctus murmured from beside me, pulling me from my somber thoughts.

I nodded. "Nyra will not get to see it for much longer. I will make sure of it."

"Now that is the spirit, princeling," Captain Jolene commented as she joined us at the prow of the *StarSeeker*.

"Quite right," Leo said approvingly from my other side. "Is everything proceeding smoothly on Rigel's end?"

"I have yet to hear otherwise." We had been coordinating closely over the last few days, and so far there had been no significant hiccups.

"Good. Shall we commence our descent?" The grizzled soldier looked to Jolene.

"Yes. So long as his magic continues to conceal us." The captain glanced at me, and I nodded.

"We will remain undetectable until the hull touches down in Lake Hesperia." I had granted Jolene's wish for all of the ships in our fleet to become undetectable to anyone not touching some part of our ships. We had chosen sunset for our approach to ensure any glow of magic that escaped could be explained away as the light of the setting sun. "Are the decoy flags raised?"

"Aye." Captain Jolene grimaced. "Who would have thought that after everything I went through to resist flying that snake's colors, I would soon return with them disgracing my masts."

Leo put a hand on her shoulder. "How fitting then, that you bring the Woman-King's demise with you?"

The captain gave a feral grin befitting any pirate, resting her hand on the hilt of her cutlass. "I like the sound of that!"

"As do we all." Noctus fingered his knives.

"All hands!" Captain Jolene cried as she turned and strode towards the helm. "Prepare to make port!"

I remained at the prow, never taking my eyes off of Astor Castle despite the wind that pushed my dark locks back from my forehead and set my cloak streaming out behind me. That was where everything had begun, and where everything would end, one way or another.

Over the last few days, I had spent every waking moment practicing my magic and swordsmanship when I was not in meetings with the others. We had gone over the plan until it had been thoroughly ingrained in everyone's minds. Over hours of rigorous discussion and debate, we had also come up with contingency plans for every scenario we could imagine. Still, I was a mess of nerves. If we lost the element of surprise...we would be in big trouble.

"Though darkness falls..." Noctus put a hand on my shoulder in a rare gesture of affection.

I smiled, chuckling to myself at how well the quiet man could read me. "Still the stars find their way."

"And so will we." He gave my shoulder a reassuring squeeze. It felt strange to be the one on the receiving end of that comforting statement.

"Thank you, Noctus. For everything." I felt my nerves settle, at least for the moment.

I was not doing this alone. I needed to have faith in those who had put their faith in me. After all, these people had become like family to me. And family protected family.

Soon, we had flown past the castle and made for Lake Hesperia, whose calm waters glimmered like a sea of gold thanks to the sunset. I heard Captain Jolene give the command, and the wind lessened as the ship slowed to a hover, and then began to descend. The other four ships in our fleet quickly followed suit.

We set down gently, and the ship rocked as it settled into the water. The waves lapped against the hull, and my magic made it appear as if our fleet were emerging from a thick blanket of golden mist as the sails filled and we coasted to the docks.

I scanned the surrounding area nervously, searching for the gleam of beady black eyes or the flicker of magic that signified a tribesman was nearby. The only one I sensed was several streets away, and out of sight. I sighed with relief. Rigel had reported that around sunset was when most of them headed to the taverns for a meal. But just to be safe, he had organized a handful of distractions on the opposite side of the city to keep them occupied for this exact moment.

Jolene's crew quickly dropped the anchor and threw out the ropes, quickly securing the ship to its moorings. In a few moments, it would appear as if these ships had been here the whole time.

As the gangplank clacked against the wooden boards of the dock, a handful of shadows detached themselves from the nearest cluster of warehouses and made for the *StarSeeker*. Alarm spiked through me for an instant before I recognized the lead man's sword. With a grin I pulled on my hood and strode down the gangplank, Noctus and Leo right behind me.

I embraced my brother-in-arms and clapped him on the shoulder. Under his hood, I could see that there were dark shadows beneath his turquoise eyes, but his tired smile was genuine.

"Welcome back, all of you," Rigel said warmly.

"Glad to be back," I replied.

"And with friends!"

"Five ships full," Leo said glibly.

"Marvelous. Each of us will lead one group to the safehouses we have been setting up." Rigel gestured to the four behind him, who I recognized as guild members—including Sirius, Nova and Castor.

"What are *they* doing here?" I hissed, my nerves returning. "You three should still be at the lake house!"

"This is our home too, and we want to fight for it!" Nova protested hotly. She had that stubborn set to her chin that always meant trouble. "And we will do whatever it takes to save Astrid!"

I scowled. "How am I supposed to focus on saving her when I am busy worrying about you?!"

Rigel glanced around nervously. "We can have this discussion later. For now, break everyone into small groups and follow your guides one group at a time. And make sure to keep your faces covered!"

He tugged the hood of my cloak down even lower over my face with an exasperated sigh, and I grinned. It was good to be back.

"Rigel, take Orion and a few of the pirates back to the guildhouse first. I will show the guides which ships are ours." Leo gestured for the cloaked four to follow him, and led them towards the other ships.

At my signal, a handful of Jolene's crew scurried down the gangplank to join us. Rigel turned on his heel and led the way back into the maze of streets and alleys that I knew like the back of my hand.

But as we moved through the streets, I found myself clenching my jaw in anger. A handful of my people lined each street, bundled in layers of warm clothing and with bags stuffed with personal belongings. They slumped against the walls, their dirty faces downcast. Gaunt mothers clutched skinny children in their arms, and only the occasional cough or sneeze broke the eerie silence.

"This is far worse than I imagined," I said in a low tone to Rigel. "I know you reported that the tribesmen had been commandeering houses, but to see so many out on the streets..."

Rigel nodded. "The last two weeks have been brutal. To make matters worse, Nyra has raised the taxes so high that most of the shops have closed their doors. No one can afford to buy food, let alone bribe the tribesmen to find another's house to steal instead."

I scowled. "No wonder you were having so much trouble finding housing for everyone."

"It has certainly been a challenge." He grimaced. "And it does not help matters that no one can leave."

"What do you mean, no one can leave?"

"Just this morning, Nyra announced that people are no longer allowed to leave to go to other towns. She has erected barricades at all of the gates out of the city. Of course, tribesmen can still travel through them freely," Rigel said bitterly.

"I suppose her tax base was shrinking far too rapidly with so many people fleeing her tyranny," I muttered darkly. "But that is just one more reason why Nova and Castor should not be here." I leveled an accusatory look at Rigel.

"Have *you* tried arguing with that little redhead?" He threw his hands up in exasperation. "She is more stubborn than a mule, and can talk circles around you to boot!"

Despite myself, I chuckled. "Still, I would feel better knowing they were safe."

"You and me both." Rigel nodded. "But they do have a point: this is their home too, and it is their family the tyrant is targeting. If they stayed idle and safe while we fought for our lives, it would drive them mad."

I ran a hand through my hair and sighed. "While I do understand that, I now have three more people to worry about when I cannot afford distractions."

"Rigel and I will keep a close eye on them," Noctus offered. "We should be able to keep them occupied with creating batches of remedies and antidotes inside the guildhouse, and away from most of the danger."

I smiled at them both gratefully. "I would appreciate that."

As we made our way to the guildhouse, the effects of Nyra's regime were clear to see. Most of the shops in the merchant district were closed, their windows shuttered. Flowers wilted in every window box, and trash littered the streets. Some people had cobbled together make-shift shelters out of blankets and crates. And while those structures might help now, during early fall, they would do little to keep their inhabitants warm during the coming winter.

"It would seem most of the cleaning staff have quit or fled," I muttered.

"Yes. And most people would not risk catching the attention of a patrol to keep things nice." Rigel took the last few turns to the guildhouse and gave the familiar knock on the door.

Despite our dire situation, I could not help but smile as the familiar wooden door swung open on silent hinges and we were all hurriedly ushered inside. I took a deep breath, appreciating the musty smell of old wood and fresh herbs that floated in the air. I had not realized how much I missed this place.

But it felt good to be back.

Once the door had been firmly shut and bolted once more, and the sailors who had silently accompanied us were directed to some of our many guest rooms, Rigel turned to Noctus and me.

"I know you must be tired, but there is much to discuss, and for me to report to you." He smiled ruefully, and said with a little bow, "But before all that, let me be the first to welcome you both home."

10

Orion

"Now that everyone is here, we can begin." Rigel steepled his fingers seriously as he scanned the room.

What used to be our dining room had been transformed into our war room. Two tables had been pushed together to form one long table, and as many chairs as we could fit bristled around it like the spines of a porcupine. Estelle's drawings on the walls had been covered with massive maps that had red dots to mark the locations of known tribesmen hotspots, and blue dots to represent our safe houses and allies.

There were still far too many red dots for my liking, even after our recent influx of new allies.

I sat at the head of the table, while Rigel stood directly opposite me, in front of the most detailed and up-to-date map of the castle and its surrounding area. Sirius, Leo, Noctus, Regis, Raiden, Birken, Jolene, and the other four starship captains lined the sides of the table. Seeing the leaders of all of my allies here helped to ease the near-constant sense of foreboding in the pit of my stomach.

This was not going to be easy, especially now that Nyra and her people were so entrenched in the castle. But at least now we had a much better chance of success together than I had had alone just a month ago.

"Dissent amongst the people has been growing exponentially, aided in no small part by those loyal to Orion and Hyperion," Rigel began. "Our allies among the common folk have been spreading rumors of Orion's exaggerated death and subsequent return to health."

"I imagine the displacement of thousands of families has helped," Sirius added drily.

"Precisely." Rigel nodded. "Ace, a nearby tavern keeper, has been particularly instrumental in spreading this rumor, as well as collecting helpful information on the schedules and positions of the patrols. And Zale has been feeding us information as well."

I smiled, happy to hear my old friends were doing well. I should have known Ace would be more vocal than anyone when it came to opposing such heavy-handed brutality. And I was glad to hear Zale had avoided being imprisoned with the rest of the counselors and high-level staff.

"I see. Now that the people have a figure to rally behind, that brings them hope of a return to a more peaceful life and has inspired them to take greater risks," rumbled Commander Regis, stroking his short beard.

"It is a good tactic to boost morale and gather momentum for our movement," Leo agreed.

Captain Jolene shot a bemused glance at the two Harlandish soldiers and their near-identical thought processes.

"I am confused. Were the people of Astoria unaware of their prince before this?" Raiden gave me a questioning look.

"When Nyra carried out her plot to overthrow the king, she cut Prince Sterling with a poisoned blade," Rigel explained with a grimace. "While we managed to escape with the prince and deliver Astrid's newly-minted antidote to him, Nyra took the opportunity to seize control of the castle and the country. She quickly declared both the king and prince dead by her own hand."

"And you did nothing to dispel this untruth?" Birken pressed in a borderline mocking tone.

"We needed to stall for time," Noctus cut in softly. "It was more advantageous for us to let Nyra and everyone else believe Sterling was dead. It afforded us the time we needed to recover, regroup, and seek allies."

The two druids reluctantly nodded. Commander Regis gave an understanding grunt.

"But now we are ready to make our move," I said, steering the conversation back in the right direction. "Hence why those loyal to me have been spreading the news of my much-exaggerated demise."

"Precisely. Now, my spies within the royal guard have reported to me that the tyrant is conspiring with the witches—which is in line with what transpired in the Druidlands," Sir Rigel continued, nodding to me and the two druids. "However, they seem to be working on something beyond simply deploying the covens to attack Harland and Sylvaine."

I leaned forward in my chair, concern whispering through me. Astoria had little knowledge of the capabilities of the witches, since we had had so little contact with them so far. From what I had read, however, they were quite the force to be reckoned with. "Have your spies any clue what they might be plotting?"

The knight shook his head. "It is a secret they guard closely. That, alongside a couple of other crucial pieces of information, are the main reasons we have waited so long to make our move."

"You mentioned that Nyra has been stockpiling liquid starlight and stardust, but not granting any wishes, so far as you could tell," Noctus mused thoughtfully. "Do we have any idea why?"

"It is not as if she is incapable of using my mother's amulet to grant wishes. And I doubt she is selfless enough to sacrifice her own life in an attempt to revive the oases of the Desertlands," I said bitterly.

"Have you ever known the witches to use stardust or starlight in their hexes?" Noctus asked the druids and the Harlanders.

They looked thoughtful for a moment, but then shook their heads.

"They do not need stardust to make their brooms fly," Commander Regis said. "Or to power their attacks."

"And although witches tend to covet the power of fallen stars, I do not believe they have ever attempted to utilize stardust or starlight before, since it does not mix well with their own magic," Raiden added.

"Especially since using starsteel to boost the effectiveness of those substances would render their hexes harmless." Birken folded his brawny arms over his chest.

I frowned thoughtfully. "What if they found a way to corrupt starsteel?"

Every pair of eyes turned to me.

"Like the strange starsteel that was used to seal Adelaide's magic," Noctus said quietly.

I nodded. "They may have more tricks up their sleeves than we give them credit for. When that hag of a headwitch tried to put those corrupted starsteel manacles on my wrists, my connection to my magic was severed so long as the metal touched my skin." I shuddered at the memory.

"If they had a lot of that material, I think we would have seen it commonly used," Captain Jolene mused. The other captains murmured in assent.

"Hopefully, that means it is very difficult to make, and that they will not possess very much of it," Sir Rigel agreed. "But if the witches have it, then it is safe to assume that Nyra does, as well. Therefore, we should have several measures in place to counter this corrupted starsteel."

"Absolutely." I took a deep breath, and looked at Rigel. "Can your spies confirm if Astrid is...whether she..." A lump rose in my throat, the words refusing to pass my lips.

Rigel's piercing blue eyes softened. "She is still alive." I let out a silent breath. "One of the guards slipped into the kitchens a few times, and noticed that a scullery maid is in charge of bringing regular meals to the dungeons. Another who was posted to guard the door managed to catch a glimpse of her."

"Good." I fought a mental battle, wanting to rush in boldly to save Astrid this instant, sword drawn and magic at the ready. But if I knew anything about Nyra, that was exactly the sort of thing she would be expecting. No, as much as I hated to wait another instant, my best chance of successfully rescuing Astrid and retaking the castle were only possible with a careful, calculated approach. We needed more information, and a little more time to set all of the pieces into motion. I just had to pray to the stars above that Astrid could hold on just a little longer.

"What would you have us do, Prince Sterling?" Sir Rigel prompted gently.

I looked around at all of my gathered allies and squared my shoulders. They had entrusted their lives to me, and I was not about to throw them away with a hasty attack. "Here is what we are going to do."

I stood from my seat and joined Rigel in front of the map. "Before we make our assault on the castle, we are going to systematically weaken their defenses while we acquire the information we still need. First, we are going to have unmarked groups of soldiers attack and raid any and all supplies coming into or out of the castle. A hungry enemy is a weakened enemy."

I looked at Commander Regis, and he gave me a wolfish grin. "I take it I will be leading my soldiers in this endeavor?"

"Yes. Steal whatever you can and injure as many tribesmen as possible."

"Injure? Not kill?" He frowned. "Look, Your Highness, wars are not a bloodless affair. You are delusional if you believe you can retake your kingdom like that."

I smiled patiently. "Wounded soldiers will need to be tended to and fed, pulling more tribesmen off of patrols and further straining their resources."

The Commander gave a bark of laughter and slapped his side before he dipped his head to me. "Forgive me for underestimating you, Your Highness. You make a most formidable enemy indeed."

Even Leo chuckled.

I turned to the druids. "In addition to these raids, I intend to have their guards shooting at ghosts long before we make our move."

Birken grinned. "Oh, this is going to be quite enjoyable."

Raiden nodded sagely. "We shall ask the birds to peck at them during the day, and the bats to swoop at them during the night. The rodents within the castle shall spoil their stored food and chew through the bowstrings of the archers."

"Excellent. We want them tired, weak, and scared. That way, when we strike, we will have as few casualties as possible on our side." I nodded approvingly.

"Not to mention replacing all of those weapons and supplies will cost a pretty penny," Leo added.

"I like the way you think, Prince Sterling. My king is sure to want to establish a more formal alliance with you once we have sent the Woman-King packing back to her precious desert," Commander Regis said, his sharp eyes regarding me approvingly.

"Many thanks, Commander. I welcome such an alliance whole-heartedly," I replied. Perhaps I could help the Harlandish King revitalize his economy and make it possible to phase out slavery entirely in that kingdom. But that was a problem for another day.

"And I will ensure our allies within the castle know what to expect, without drawing any undue attention to themselves," Rigel added. "Once we have the rest of the information we need and have established a firm grip on the situation, we will be ready to strike."

"When that day comes, the support of the starship captains will be crucial." I nodded to each of them in turn.

"We will be ready to provide support from the air," Captain Jolene confirmed. "Our comet cannons will be primed and ready."

"Thank you. I know I can count on all of you," I said with a warm smile. "Stars willing, we will all be reconvening in a reclaimed castle within a fortnight."

Sir Rigel clapped me on the shoulder. "It is good to have you back, Prince Sterling. Now, let us get to work!"

11

Astrid

"I am here with the druid's meal." The scullery girl's voice echoed faintly down the stone corridor. She still refused to tell me her name.

"Get on with it then," the guard said irritably as I heard his keys jangle against the iron door. Light footsteps hurried through as the hinges squealed, and the girl soon appeared outside my cell.

"I brought you an extra potato—do not let the guards see." She glanced nervously over her shoulder and kept her tone low. She pulled out my little pouch of stardust and added a pinch of the precious powder to the thin soup with deft fingers.

"Thank you." I gave her a weak smile as my eyes fell on the wooden tray she carried, my mouth already watering in anticipation—not for the food, but for the stardust sprinkled on it.

She nodded and pushed the little tray into my cell before scurrying away. Before the dungeon's iron door had even clanged shut once more, I had pulled the tray to the back of the cell with me. Despite the cold bite of the stone at my back, I preferred to stay as far out of reach as possible—just in case. If any spiteful tribesmen wanted to hit me, they would have to open the door and come in to do it. That way, I could attempt another escape—not that any such opportunity had presented itself yet.

I forced myself to slowly spoon the thin soup into my mouth, savoring the small bit of warmth that still lingered in the liquid. I could feel the soothing effects of the stardust almost immediately, and I sighed in relief. I had had to use the last of my own secret supply earlier in the day, during one of my worst seizures so far. Now, only my daily meal could combat the constant ache of pain radiating from my core.

Reverently, I broke open the baked potato and breathed in the warm steam that wafted up. It was much warmer than the soup, and far more filling. Oh, how I missed being able to cook meals for myself and my guildmates!

I missed Sirius' lively jokes and Estelle's tinkling laugh. I missed Noctus' quiet smiles and Celeste's witty comebacks. I even missed Orion's nearly always empty chair at the table. But most of all, I missed the warmth of my home and the people who filled it.

Tears pricked the back of my eyes, and I drew my knees up to my chin. It took a great effort to keep my thoughts from spiraling into despair and hopelessness. I had to hold on to the hope that I would get the chance to see them all again—if only for a moment.

An odd tapping noise startled me from my thoughts, and I looked up from my half-eaten potato to see a raven staring at me from only a few feet away. I flinched, glancing around in confusion. How on earth had a bird managed to get into the dungeon? There were no windows here!

"Hello, there," I said softly to the bird, and it hopped closer. "How did you get in here?"

I furrowed my brow. And how had the tribesmen not noticed its presence?

The raven cocked its head and croaked, and I realized it must have been looking at the potato, not me. I broke off a tiny bit of the fluffy white insides and held it out to the bird, my palm flat. Its iridescent feathers glimmered beautifully with hues of violet and indigo in the flickering torchlight.

It ruffled its feathers, as if in annoyance. To my utter shock and confusion, the raven suddenly began to stretch and grow taller. Inky black feathers retreated into smooth skin, and within moments Adelaide stood where the raven had just been.

"I am not here to take your potato," Adelaide said stiffly, but not unkindly. "Though I appreciate the offer."

My jaw dropped.

"Adelaide?!" I croaked. "What the—Adelaide?"

"Ssh! Not so loud!" She glanced towards the dungeons' entrance, but no one raised the alarm. "That is my name—no need to wear it out." Despite her soft chuckle at my expression, something seemed off.

"Was that a transformation hex?" I swallowed nervously. "I thought the tales of witches turning people into toads were only stories mothers used to scare young children into behaving!" Now that I thought about it, I had seen such hexes used during the battle at Pyrcairn—but I had been trying to block out those memories since my capture.

Adelaide grimaced. "Those hexes are real enough—I have been subjected to them enough times. Those are not permanent and wear off over time. But unlike the others, my maternal line has always had the ability to change our forms into that of a raven at will."

I stared at her as I tried to process this confusing little tidbit. Then my eyes widened. "Is that how you slipped into my cell last time? When you fed me some stardust?"

Adelaide nodded. "Yes. These bars pose no problem for me." She crouched down beside me.

When the witch fell silent, I examined her more closely. She was fidgeting with her hair, as if she could not keep still, and there was a tightness around her mouth and red eyes that told me she was worried about something.

"You seem upset, Adelaide, and everyone seems jumpy and on edge." She looked at me in surprise. "What is wrong?"

She bit her lip, a habit I realized belatedly she must have picked up from me, since I had never seen Helga or the Headwitch do such a thing. Her hands started to shake. I hesitated, wondering that I still felt the instinct to comfort her, after everything she had done. But when I placed my own hand over hers, she finally looked at me.

"Oh, well...the rebels have been harassing Nyra's patrols and raiding her supply lines. Every night, another storehouse is hit. There are even rumors—" she broke off, glancing at me nervously.

I perked up. People were resisting Nyra? "What rumors?"

Uncertainty flickered across her face, but after a moment, she seemed to come to some sort of decision. "Rumors have been circulating that Prince Sterling is still alive, and that he is here—leading the resistance."

My heart soared. Orion was *here*? Did that mean Queen Rowena had decided to ally with him after all?

"He came back," I breathed. Would I really get to see him again? Could I see everyone I loved one more time? And did I dare to hope that my aunt or Orion had discovered a cure for me in the meantime?

Adelaide nodded slowly. "He is most likely near." She looked down, her voice dropping to a hoarse whisper. "But he should have stayed away."

"What? Why?!" I exclaimed, alarmed at the look in the witch's eyes. I shook her shoulders gently. "What are you not telling me?!"

She shook her head, pressing her lips together. After a shaky inhale, she breathed out, "Astrid, you were right—about *everything*. Headwitch Brunhilde never had any intention of keeping her word to me. She has only been using me this whole time. She was never going to free me." The witch tugged angrily at the corrupted starsteel choker around her neck. "And the things they are planning..."

Adelaide swallowed, and my alarm and confusion grew. "Tell me everything. From the beginning."

She looked at the floor, but after a moment of hesitation, she nodded. "When I went to speak with the Headwitch, I overheard her and Helga conversing when they thought I was asleep in my room." She slowly raised her eyes to mine, as if she carried the weight of the world on her shoulders. "The grand hex Nyra has commissioned, the one I have been helping to prepare, which requires an obscene amount of stardust and liquid starlight—its purpose is to restore the oases in the southern Desertlands."

I frowned. "Even with the amulet, I thought it was impossible to grant such a wish—even with the addition of another kind of magic."

Adelaide nodded slowly. "It *is*. There is not nearly enough stardust or mountain herbs to make it feasible."

"Then how...?" I felt a dawning sense of unease.

"She is going to power the majority of the hex-supported wish with the lives of every Astorian within the city."

I felt the blood drain from my face. I shook my head, unable to comprehend the depths of Nyra's depravity. "No."

"Yes. And once I have outlived my usefulness, Headwitch Brunhilde is going to seal the rest of my powers and sacrifice me as well," the witch said bitterly.

I buried my face in trembling hands. It was a trap far more vile and horrifying than I could have imagined. If Orion had returned to save me, to save his kingdom, with all of our guildmates and a small army of allies in tow, then every single one of their lives were in mortal danger at this very moment.

My head snapped up, my eyes blazing with helpless anger, and I was ready to lay into Adelaide for baiting this appalling trap and helping to prepare this heinous ritual. But instead of looking defiant or defensive, she just looked...miserable. Her head was bowed, her ebony hair falling over her face like a curtain, as if she was waiting to accept punishment from me.

All at once, the fury drained out of me, and I dropped my hands to my lap. She was also a victim of Nyra's scheming. We had both been betrayed by someone we trusted now. And while I felt a little vindicated that she now knew how it felt, that would do little to get me out of this cell so I could warn Orion.

Unless...

I looked at her, really looked at her. Adelaide had come to me, the person she had betrayed, for comfort. She had clearly had some measure of doubt about her actions before, but now that doubt was gone. And she was positioned perfectly to do something about it.

"So what are you going to *do?*" I asked sharply.

She raised her head, startled out of her miserable thoughts. "What?"

"Are you going to let them seal your powers and sacrifice you? And every person who welcomed you into our family?" I narrowed my eyes, searching for that spark of strength I knew was buried in her heart. "Are you *really* going to let them get away with that? After everything else they have put you through?"

Adelaide scowled, but did not say anything. I could tell my words were hitting home, but she still looked despondent.

"And do you think dying helplessly with the rest of us will somehow absolve you of your guilt about what you did to me? To Rafe?"

Her eyes hardened. "That would be better than going on alone! Living on as an exile is a fate worse than death. I swore I would never...I would never end up like my mother!"

I smiled internally, and went in for the kill. "Rafe is still alive. If you give up now, he may just end up dying along with the rest of us."

Her ruby eyes widened. "What? No, I saw him—"

"You saw him get pushed into the wild magic in the heart of the Sacred Willow. Just before you captured me, I saw him come out—as a man, instead of a wolf."

"Are you certain?!" She grabbed my shoulders, her eyes desperately searching mine for even the slightest shred of a lie.

"His eyes remained golden, but his ears were pointed and his hair was blonde—like a druid's," I confirmed.

Her eyes narrowed in suspicion. "Why are you only telling me this *now?!*" There was an undercurrent of hope and heartache in her voice.

"Because I was still angry with you for condemning me to a lonely death, away from the man I love with all of my heart. The same way you love Rafe."

Adelaide slowly released my shoulders, looking stricken. Her eyes glistened in the torchlight with pent-up emotion. Understanding seemed to settle around her shoulders like a cloak. "I suppose I cannot blame you for that."

She looked away again, her shoulders drooping. I scooted closer to her, and said softly, "If Orion has returned, then I have little doubt that Rafe came with him." Finally, her red eyes found mine, a spark of tortured hope in their ruby depths.

"Astrid—" she said, her eyes welling with tears. "Astrid, I am so sorry for what I did to you and Orion and everyone else."

I sat up straight, shocked. I had never seen the witch cry—or *any* witch cry, for that matter. Witches had never been known to apologize, either.

"Thank you for saying that." It felt like some of my lingering resentment towards her began to melt away. I put a hand on her back as she sobbed quietly, and moved it in soothing circles, just as my mother had once done for me. Perhaps, if I lived to see the other side of this disastrous situation, I might be able to truly and fully forgive her.

"How much time do we have left before Nyra goes through with her plan?" My mind turned back to the problem at hand. There was no way I could give up now, not when I knew everyone I loved was in mortal danger.

Adelaide sniffled, and roughly dried her eyes on her black sleeve. They were puffy and rimmed with red, but they had never looked more determined. "Two weeks, at best. More, if I can manage to undo some of the progress I have made."

"That is not a lot of time." I bit my lip, thinking. I needed to have Adelaide get in contact with Sir Rigel. How many of the castle's original guards were still loyal to him, to our cause? But even if she *did* make contact, no one from the guild would ever trust her again. They would assume she was setting them up.

A cruel grin bent the witch's lips. "I will also do everything in my power to drive a wedge between Brunhilde, Helga, Nyra, and her harem of warriors. That should buy us more time."

I nodded absently, fingering the star-shaped pendant around my neck. Its rough facets had become as familiar as my own face over the last few weeks. "Good idea. We need to delay the ritual as long as we can."

"It might take some time, but I will try to steal the amulet," Adelaide declared, squaring her shoulders. "Without that, the whole ritual would fall apart."

"You must get it away from her at all costs," I agreed, my fingers closing over my pendant. I was reluctant to do what I knew needed to be done. "Does she know you can turn into a raven?"

The witch shook her head. "No. Only you and Rafe know."

I smiled to myself. "You know, I always wondered why you seemed so unconcerned when you were hanging off the side of the ship during that storm. Now I know—you were never in any real danger to begin with." I chuckled. "Though that did not seem to occur to Rafe."

She smiled softly.

"Use that secret to your advantage, then. Steal it as a witch, a maid, a bird—however you can. And in the meantime..." I trailed off, my hand tightening.

Adelaide raised an eyebrow, glancing at my fisted hand. Her lips parted in surprise when I reverently unclasped the necklace and held it out to her. The many facets of the carved star glittered in the flickering torch light.

"Take this," I ordered around the lump in my throat.

Adelaide shook her head and pushed my hands away. "Absolutely not! That is your only lifeline! I have no idea why you have yet to use it, but you should! You should make a wish for that stupid curse to be undone this instant! I did *not* risk a beating so you could keep that thing just to give it away."

I held it over my heart for another moment before I held it out to her once more. "Find Sir Rigel at the guildhouse. He will likely have measures in place should you return, but once Orion sees this necklace, they should believe you."

"They will think I stole it from you, regardless." I smiled at her frankness, happy to see how wise to the world she had become in such a short time.

"It cannot be stolen. It will always return to its owner. The only way for it to change owners is for it to be given willingly. Orion knows this—it was how his mother designed it." He had revealed this secret to me long before he gave me the necklace, when I had asked him to hide it in a secure location in case Nyra caught wind of its existence.

Adelaide slowly reached out her hands with trembling fingers, and took the pendant as if it were the most precious thing in the world. I felt a great sense of loss when the last links of the necklace left my hands, like she took a part of me with it.

"I swear that I will return it to you," Adelaide said solemnly. Her ruby eyes never wavered. "And I will do whatever it takes to make up for my past mistakes."

12

Orion

"F ire at will." I held up a hand, and watched with grim satisfaction from my hidden vantage point on the roof as smoking bundles of herbs were tossed down onto the street below.

I only saw the shock and distress on the five tribesmens' faces for an instant before our homemade smoke bombs exploded, veiling their figures in a dense mist. The wooden horse-drawn wagon, laden with stardust, foodstuffs, and other supplies that they were guarding, disappeared just as quickly, until only a vague, rectangular shadow marked its position. Beside me, Aria drew back the bowstring on her weapon, firing into the smoke before her target had a chance to react.

On the rooftops across from us, I watched Noctus and Birken do the same. Grunts of pain and the panicked neigh of the horse told me that four of the men had been hit.

"Get that nag moving!" yelled one of the tribesmen between coughs. "Those damned rebels are here!"

The crack of a whip sounded in the still night air. But then I heard the abused animal collapsing onto the cobblestones as the tranquilizer Castor had prepared sent the horse to sleep.

An inspired string of curses rang out, as more thuds echoed off the cobblestones, and the lone, conscious tribesman bolted out of the smokescreen and fled towards the castle. It seemed our reputation preceded us.

At my signal, Birken raised a hand, and a sudden gust of wind cleared the smoke, sending it safely into the dark night sky. I, along with the rest of my small group, slid down our hidden ladders and jogged over to the motionless wagon.

"Quick, before he comes back with the nearest patrol," I said as I reached for the small leather pouch at my waist.

Aria nodded and copied my movements. We quickly threw handfuls of stardust onto the horse and wagon, and within moments they began to slowly float upwards, until they hovered about a foot off of the ground. My hair glowed with silvery light, and I made no attempt to dim it. It was my way of telling my people that their prince was fighting for them, and I knew the few Astorians who happened to see me during these raids would spread the word.

At first, Commander Regis had voiced his concern of spies amongst the common people, who might report us to Nyra. That had worried me as well, but it was a risk I felt we needed to take. Now that more and more people had seen through Nyra's lies, there were fewer on her side.

We *had* had one close call, right after we first began the raids. But once the supplies we stole began making their way into the neediest hands, we had no similar incidents.

"We should take this one to the warehouse," Noctus said in a hushed whisper. "None of the safehouses have room."

I nodded. "Scout ahead and distract or take out any patrols on the way. We will follow as quickly as we are able."

"Understood." Noctus scaled a ladder and took off across the rooftops, moving as silently as a wraith.

Birken, Sirius and I began to push and pull the floating wooden wagon and horse along the street, while Aria walked beside us, her bow nocked and ready. A thin sheen of green coated the tip of the arrow; Nova's newest creation. It was a hallucinogenic herb that, when added to Castor's tranquilizer, would keep the tribesmen struck with it out of service for at least ten days.

Hopefully, by the time the effects faded, we would already have them locked in the dungeons after retaking the castle.

"Good job tonight, Aria," I murmured as she drew near. "Your marksmanship has improved remarkably."

A wide grin lit up her face, but she kept her eyes roving for threats. "Thank you. And thank you for letting me join the raids—I am glad to be useful."

"We need every pair of skilled hands we can muster," I said as I steered us around a corner.

We fell silent, and soon passed a group of snoring tribesmen heaped into a pile against the wall. We shuffled past them, though Aria took a moment to liberate them of their coin and weapons, and added those to our wagon. After walking down a few more streets, we arrived at a small warehouse, not too far from Lake Hesperia, and were quickly ushered inside by Noctus.

"Good job taking out that patrol." I nodded in thanks.

"It was easy with the apprentices' tranquilizers." Noctus had taken to the substance with gusto, and now coated all of his blades with it.

The doors were closed and barred the moment the tip of the horse's nose cleared them. A pair of Harlandish soldiers joined us, helping to move our burden over to a far corner of the half-full space, between towering stacks of crates and burlap sacks of potatoes. An Astorian sympathizer had lent us use of his company's warehouse, and we were more than happy to give him some of the horses and wagons we captured to thank him.

"Stand clear," I ordered, once we had the load where we wanted it and the horse had been detached from its harness and placed over a bed of hay.

After I was sure everyone had stepped away from it, I held out my hand and used my magic to sense the particles of stardust that remained. Once I had a firm grasp on them, I clenched my fist and *pulled.* As the bits of stardust detached from the horse and the wagon and streamed into my open pouch, both objects slowly lowered down to the floor.

I closed off the pouch and let the final particles of stardust absorb into my skin. I had a feeling I would be needing that little boost of energy to get through the rest of the night.

"Life became much easier after you learned that little trick," Sirius grunted.

I chuckled. "No kidding."

The first time we had used stardust to temporarily make a stolen wagon float, we had no idea when it would wear off. Late in the night, the merchant had practically suffered a small heart attack when the horseless wagon had suddenly come crashing down, fearing the tribesmen had discovered his illicit activities and broken down the door.

Fortunately, after some experimentation, I had figured out that I could control stardust using my magic. And after a little more practice, I could withdraw the stardust slowly enough to set the load down gently.

"Shall we check on the druids and the soldiers, and hear how their missions have been going?" Sirius suggested.

I stifled a yawn. "Good idea."

We spent the next couple of hours at three of the safehouses, where a large chunk of our allies were housed. At the first one, Raiden reported that operations were going smoothly. The druids took shifts, either accompanying soldiers on raids, or using their magic to have birds, bats, and mice harass the tribesmen and damage their supplies. At the second, Commander Regis showed us the sizable piles of supplies they had pillaged from the patrols and supply lines they had attacked. And at the third, Captain Jolene shared with me the revisions to our battle strategy that she, Leo, and Raiden had been tirelessly working on. The starships were now fully supplied, and on standby to launch the moment I gave the word.

When Sirius had to elbow me awake for the third time, I decided to call it a night. The chilly breeze in my face perked me up on the way back to the Guildhouse, and I rubbed my tired eyes as we entered.

"Aria, glad to have you back!" Nova tackled her in a hug, with Castor trailing at her side like a shadow. "Were you hurt at all?"

Aria grinned. "Not even a scratch! And I managed to take out a tribesman tonight!" She brandished her bow proudly.

"Great job! Do you think I need to make any tweaks to the herbal composition? How long did it take before he passed out? Was he—"

"Aria has had a long night, and needs to get some rest," I broke in, my lips curving at the slightly bewildered look on Aria's face and the excited look on Nova's. "As do you. Go get ready for bed; you can ask her all your questions in the morning."

Nova pouted, but said dutifully, "Yes, Orion."

I winked at Castor, and he grinned back, as he ushered the pair towards their room. I could hear Nova start up again, moments before the door shut. At least those three were getting along so well. Almost *too* well; I worried about the sorts of mischief they might get into once this was all over.

"All went well, I take it?" Sir Rigel asked as he waved Noctus and me into what we had dubbed our "war room." Sirius went about reporting the night's activities to the others.

"All according to plan." I noticed that the dark circles under his eyes rivaled my own.

"Any progress on contacting Astrid?" My chest tightened at the thought of what she must be enduring, even now.

Rigel's smile faded, and I knew his answer before he spoke. "Not yet. My spies have been unable to safely reach her; she is under constant guard."

I sighed in frustration and ran a hand through my hair. "At least we will have an idea of where to look. But we cannot delay for much longer."

"I know. I propose we—"

Sirius burst through the door. "Orion, Rigel—that traitorous witch has returned. Adelaide is at the door."

Rigel and I stood so quickly that our chairs fell over.

"How many tribesmen did she bring—" Rigel began, already reaching for his sword.

But Sirius was shaking his head. "She appears to be alone. None of our scouts are reporting tribesmen anywhere near here."

"Do not forget that the Headwitch can teleport." Noctus rose, his face grim. "Put everyone on high alert—"

I strode to the door, rage darkening my visage and turning the world red around the edges. All of the grief and fury I had been suppressing bubbled up to the surface, the memory of Astrid's confused and terrified face, right before she was taken, filling my mind. I could hear the phantom ticking of a clock, counting down how much time I had left to get to her before the druid's curse took her from me forever.

I was vaguely aware of the others scrambling to get out of my way, but my focus was trained on the ajar front door. Pale skin and long ebony hair came into view, and before I even knew what I was doing, I had wrenched the door all the way open.

Adelaide looked just as I remembered, and her mouth formed a small O at the look on my face. Her face paled even further, and she held up her hands. "Orion, I came to help—"

Heedless of the danger or the hands that tried to hold me back, I fisted the coarse fabric of her black dress just below her collarbone and slammed her against the wall. The breath left her lungs. "Where is she?!"

"Astrid is—" Adelaide stammered as she tried to reach towards her neck.

"What have you done with her?!" I shook her for emphasis. I had become more desperate to reach her with every futile attempt by our spies, and here the answer had walked up to us on her own two feet.

I was not about to let this chance slip through my fingers.

Adelaide scowled, her eyes flaring crimson a moment before an invisible force barreled into my chest, forcing me back a step. I raised a hand as I called on my own magic, letting the starlight spilling through the door begin to take form around her like the bars of a cage.

The witch's eyes widened in fear and surprise, but before any more magic could be used, Nova darted in between us and delivered a stinging slap to Adelaide. But then she turned right around and slapped me, too.

The shock snapped me out of my rage, and I looked down at the fiery little redhead with incredulity. My ego hurt far more than my cheek, and I ran a hand through my now-glowing hair. I noticed belatedly that both Rigel and Sirius were posed as if they had been about to try and restrain me.

"Knock it off, you magic-wielding morons, before you attract every patrol in the district!" she hissed. "Adelaide, that was for stealing my master away from me after everything we did for you. And Orion, I expected better from my future king!"

I clenched my jaw, feeling chagrined. Nova was right. A king does not let his emotions cloud his judgment—especially when the lives of his loved ones hang in the balance.

"How about we have this...discussion inside?" Castor suggested quietly from behind us.

I nodded tersely and released my hold on my magic, capping it so that my hair and eyes returned to normal. Adelaide nodded as well, but I did not take my eyes off of her for an instant.

Noctus ushered her into one of our smaller meeting rooms, where none of the maps marked the locations of our allies.

Adelaide's eyes flickered around the room, hopping from face to face. I frowned. Was she looking for an escape route? No, she was looking for someone. And then it clicked.

I pulled Sirius aside, and whispered, "Keep Rafe out of sight—at least for now."

He nodded and hurried off.

I followed them into the small room, closing the door behind me and standing in front of it to block any possible escape. I saw Adelaide roll her eyes, and I had to grit my teeth to stop myself from snapping at her. She sat, as did Noctus, Rigel, and Nova, who was studiously avoiding my eyes.

Adelaide looked around the room, but found no sympathetic faces. She took a deep breath and said, "I came here to tell you that I have switched sides."

I scoffed. "I will not be falling for your lies a second time."

When she reached towards her neck, Noctus and Rigel both tensed, but she simply pulled out a necklace that made me go very, very still. "Astrid told me that you would believe me if I showed you this."

"Showing us her stolen belongings was the best you could come up with, witch?" Rigel raised a disbelieving eyebrow.

Those unnerving crimson eyes never left mine.

"That pendant was enchanted in such a way that it could never be stolen, even if the owner died." The words felt heavy on my tongue, and I scowled, struggling to believe what that meant. "Astrid gave it to her freely."

Silence reigned for a beat, before Rigel slammed his hands against the table. "The witch could have put sandberries in her food, or—"

I held up a hand, and he fell silent.

"If you truly have switched allegiances, then why did you come *alone?*" The words were quiet, deadly, but Adelaide met my gaze without flinching.

"Because security is tight, and she is too weak to travel. And if I attempted to use my magic on Astrid to help her escape, I would only fuel the curse and shorten her lifespan even further."

I considered her words. That was indeed plausible.

"What brought about this drastic change in loyalty?"

"I recently learned what Nyra and Brunhilde are plotting, and what they plan to do with me after I have outlived my usefulness." Grief flickered across her face.

"So the betrayer has been betrayed," I murmured, my eyes narrowing.

"What did you learn?" Rigel leaned forward eagerly.

Adelaide hesitated. "I would like to conduct an exchange. I will tell you everything I know, including where Astrid is being kept and how to reach her, in return for...Rafe."

"You abandoned him to his fate when you kidnapped Astrid and ran away," I snarled, angry that even now she was trying to bargain with me, holding Astrid over my head. Well, two could play at that game.

"So he *is* alive," she breathed. Relief and excitement lit up her face, the emotions raw. "Is he here? With you? I thought I felt a flicker of his magic, but I was not sure..."

I smiled internally, suddenly glad that I had allowed the druid prince to come along with us after all.

"Why should that matter to you? You have no claim over him." Adelaide's eyes narrowed, my words striking home. I finally had some leverage over her.

"I *could* just take him." Her eyes flared red.

"I *could* just kill you." My eyes glowed silver.

Rigel shot me a withering look, but I ignored him. I would never actually go through with such a threat, but after my loss of self-control earlier, Adelaide might just believe it. This was now a hostage negotiation, and I needed the witch to see me as a powerful potential threat.

Her eyes dulled to their regular hue, and I allowed mine to fade back to blue. Tension radiated through the room, so thick I could cut it with a knife. I refused to back down, to show even the tiniest hint of weakness.

"I suppose you are not as much of a soft-hearted fool as I once thought," Adelaide finally said, leaning back in her chair, and looking me over appraisingly.

"And I suppose your heart is not as black as your dress."

Adelaide blinked in surprise, then threw her head back and laughed. I crossed my arms over my chest, feeling some of the tension ease.

"You seem different. And not just because you finally learned how to wield your magic," Adelaide said, wiping at the corner of her eye. "It seems you are no longer afraid to protect what is yours. An important quality for any Headwitch—or king. I think you might just be able to pull this off."

I raised an eyebrow, somewhat surprised by the compliment. "And you seem like you have finally stopped trying to be something you are not and allowing others to dictate your life for you."

She grinned, the first true smile I had ever seen on her face. "Will you at least let me *see* Rafe? If I tell you what I know?"

"Whether he wants to see you or not is up to him. But he is free to make that choice." I uncrossed my arms and strode over to the table, bracing my hands against it as I leaned toward the turncoat witch. "So tell me what happened, starting from the moment you arrived here from the Druidlands."

Adelaide's determined gaze met mine. "I will tell you everything I know."

13

Orion

I leaned back in my chair, stunned. The room was deathly quiet as everyone tried to wrap their heads around everything Adelaide had just revealed to us.

"So that is why she is preventing anyone else from leaving. Not for taxes, or for labor, but to use their very lives as magic fodder," Rigel murmured.

"But how is she going to manage that, practically speaking? From my understanding, the user of star magic has to be physically near the person whose wish is being granted." Sirius glanced at me for confirmation, and I nodded.

That was the sole reason why I needed to find Astrid so badly. If I could grant a wish to destroy her curse from a distance, I would have done so the very moment I knew that I could. But the magic had to be guided, and I needed to be in the same room to do that. To try otherwise would be to risk the magic running wild.

"With a grand hex." Guilt clouded Adelaide's red eyes. "Headwi— I mean, Brunhilde is going to tie the lifeforce of everyone within Astoria's borders to Nyra's. Well, except for her own, Helga's, and the tribesmens', of course."

Nova gasped, a hand flying to her mouth.

"When?" Quiet rage coiled around the word. How *dare* Nyra even consider doing something so *heinous?!*

Adelaide's frank gaze met mine. "In two nights' time. I came to warn you as soon as I heard."

I stood, my heart leaping into my throat. Everyone else jumped to their feet as well. "Then we have no time to lose. Noctus, get every last detail from Adelaide, and make sure our plan is still sound. Nova, I want you, Aria and Castor producing as many antidotes and tranquilizers as you possibly can. Sirius, send out messengers to inform our allies of this new development, and tell them to prepare to execute the plan at dusk tomorrow. Rigel, put your spies on standby and then come find me."

Everyone jumped to do as I ordered, and the quiet guildhouse soon became a hive of activity, despite the late hour. I pinched the bridge of my nose and closed my eyes for a moment, knowing I was unlikely to be getting any rest tonight.

I took a deep, bracing breath, and strode over to the war room and planted myself in front of our most comprehensive map.

Everything was already in place for our assault on the castle; we would simply be executing the plan sooner than anticipated. My insides twisted with nerves, and I tried not to entertain thoughts of all the ways things could still go horribly wrong.

I clenched my hands into fists. One way or another, by this time tomorrow, I would finally be reunited with Astrid. The few weeks we had been apart felt like a small eternity. How foolish I had been to take her comforting presence for granted for so long.

But never again.

While tracing our planned route on the map, I tried to think of everything that could possibly go wrong. We would be relying on the element of surprise and using the secret tunnels that ran through the castle like a warren. I rested my hand on the hilt of my sword. Everything hinged on taking out Nyra, her harem, and the other two witches. With their leaders gone, the tribesmen would be in disarray, presenting us with the opportunity to oust them entirely.

A knock sounded on the door, drawing me from my thoughts. I turned to see Noctus standing at the entrance, with Adelaide looking over his shoulder. I walked out of the room and closed the door behind me.

"We should only need to make a few minor tweaks to our plans." Noctus gestured at Adelaide. "She was hoping to see Rafe before heading back."

I crossed my arms over my chest, my eyes drawn to the star pendant around her neck, which hung just below the corrupted starsteel choker. "Bring him out."

Noctus nodded and went to retrieve the druid.

"Do you want to have it back?" Adelaide asked, her hand finding the pendant.

"Take it back to Astrid. I would feel better knowing she has it. But...why has she not used it yet?"

The witch frowned, looking down. "I...I do not know. She did not say." She bit her lip, then continued hesitantly, "I know she has tried to escape at least once, but when that failed, she attempted to goad Helga into..." Adelaide swallowed, and finally met my eyes. "She did not want to be the reason you walked into Nyra's trap."

I worked my jaw, trying to reign in the absolute storm of emotions that admission set loose in me. That was so like Astrid.

"If you can, convince her to use it. And give her this, if you can smuggle it in." I held out a pouch of stardust to her. I had a feeling Astrid had to be running low by now. "And tell her...tell her I will see her soon."

Adelaide nodded, and eagerly took the pouch. "I have a scullery maid slipping stardust into her food, but she is nearly out. This will help her hold on until we can free her."

I blinked, surprised the witch had been that thoughtful. Perhaps she truly had turned over a new leaf.

"Rafe will see her now." Noctus reappeared, and I spotted the druid standing a few paces back down the hall.

Adelaide's eyes went round as soon as she spotted him, filled with too many emotions to name. "Rafe," she breathed.

As Adelaide went to move past me to go to him, I set a hand on her shoulder, my eyes dropping to the choker. "Help me save Astrid, and my kingdom, and I will see what I can do about removing that seal."

Something that looked dangerously like hope flickered in her eyes, and she nodded before continuing on down the hall to Rafe. I gestured to Noctus, and we returned to the war room to give them some privacy.

"Well?" I prompted.

"It will be tight, but with a few modifications, we should be able to make it in time." Noctus looked about as grim as I had ever seen him.

"Good. And Adelaide?"

"I have tasked her with getting in contact with one of our spies, and delaying the ritual magic for as long as she possibly can without giving herself away." A muscle feathered in his jaw.

"What is it?"

"Orion, this combination of magic—it has never been attempted before. There is no telling what will happen, whether it succeeds or not. I know you have learned much about your magic in a short time, but—if it comes down to it—can you control or combat that much magic power alone?" His dark eyes cut to mine.

Was I capable of something like that? Sure, I knew I could handle my own magic now, but the kind of magical power we were talking about was staggering. The magical power of every life within the city, combined with the power of the amulet and the witches, plus however much stardust and starlight Nyra had gathered on top of that? I had had a hard enough time simply granting a few back-to-back wishes that encompassed multiple people.

Would my mind simply break under that much pressure?

"Let us hope we do not have to find out," I said grimly. But in the back of my mind, I wondered how Nyra was planning to manage such a feat. Using my mother's amulet would surely help, but even that had its limits.

Or had she convinced herself that an iron will was all it would take? Had she truly considered the risks, or was she so blinded by greed and desperation that she simply did not care?

"We should bring as much extra stardust and starsteel as we can carry—just in case." Noctus clapped me on the shoulder, and I could tell he was putting on a brave face for me.

I nodded. "If all goes according to plan, we will not need it. Make your final preparations. Tomorrow, we retake the Kingdom of the Stars."

14

Astrid

A sharp clang and the sound of shouting echoed through the dungeons from the entrance. I could not see the guard from my cell, but I could hear him. He was shifting from foot to foot, as if a colony of fire ants were crawling up his pants.

If the rest of the castle was in as much of an uproar, then something big was happening. Worry clouded my mind, and I bit my lip. Was Nyra beginning her foolhardy plan? Was everyone I loved about to have their lifeforce sucked right out of them? Or were Orion and his allies already beginning their assault on the castle?

I hated being kept in the dark, with no idea what was happening.

I hoped with everything in me that Adelaide had made contact with Sir Rigel last night, and that she was able to warn them in time. The star pendant should have been enough to convince Orion, and therefore the others, that her words could be trusted. Though its absence felt like a gaping hole in my chest, like my final connection with Orion had been severed.

But even though nearly a full day had passed, I had not seen the witch since. Every time I heard a faint scratching noise, I looked around in hopes of spotting an out-of-place black bird. But every time, it was just the guard scratching an itch, or one of the other prisoners shuffling about in their cells.

Pacing in my cell would have helped ease some of the anxiety of not knowing, but I was far too weak for that. I could barely even move. Nearly all of my magic had been consumed by the curse, which now throbbed in time with my heartbeat. The amount of stardust in my daily meal had dwindled to practically nothing, and I could tell the scullery girl was trying to make it last as long as she could.

Cold, icy fear wrapped around my aching chest. Now that my certain death was fast approaching, I could not help but wish I had more time. I almost regretted holding onto the star pendant instead of using it in the hope that it might have enough magic left to save me. I knew it was foolish to hold onto it out of loneliness and the fear I would just end up wasting it. But if I *had* used it, Orion and the others would have walked blindly into Nyra's trap.

I drew my knees under my chin and rocked back and forth, trying to generate a little bit of warmth. I closed my eyes and pictured Orion's stunning blue eyes, the way they narrowed in anger when he was protecting me, and how they crinkled at the corners when he laughed. Warmth bloomed in the hollow of my chest.

That night when we had danced under the stars on the *StarSeeker* felt like far too long ago. But the memory of his touch, of his lips brushing against mine... These memories were as sharp as daggers, and more precious than stars. They sustained me, kept me holding on just a little while longer.

I dropped my head between my knees. Would I get the chance to see him again, just one last time?

Even holding on one more day felt as insurmountable as scaling the tallest peak in the Witchlands now.

The squeal of the dungeon door opening scraped against my ears, but I did not bother to raise my head. Sharp footsteps clacked against the cold stone, and came to a stop outside my cell.

"I see you have taken to your new accommodations well, *princess*," hissed the last voice I expected to hear.

I slowly raised my head, my stomach twisting into knots. Nyra stood just beyond the bars, one hand propped cockily on her hip and her chin slanted up, so that she was looking down her nose at me. Instead of her usual traditional top and skirt, she wore armor and had her scimitar strapped to her hip. It seemed she had come to gloat. But why *now*, when I had already been here for weeks? And why was she alone? Where was her harem of guards? Was there something she did not want them to hear?

When I only stared at her, Nyra shifted uncomfortably. "Well? Do you have nothing to say?"

"Should I?" I rasped. "What could we possibly have to discuss?"

Nyra seemed taken aback, and almost...disappointed. Had she come here looking for a fight? Was there some part of her that wanted to feel justified in the horrific course she had chosen?

"I thought you ought to know that my preparations are finally complete." She sneered. "And your time in this world is almost up."

I laughed, a dry, broken sort of sound. "Tell me something I do not know."

Nyra faltered. She seemed...off. Unsteady. "You should be crying, or begging me for your life!"

All of my fear melted away, leaving an empty sort of numbness, of acceptance, in its wake. After all, there was nothing else she could do to me now.

I scoffed. "As if someone who heartlessly sacrifices children would spare one dying halfling like me."

Nyra flinched. "How did you...?"

"I am cursed, not dumb." I narrowed my eyes. "After all the misery you have caused, please do not tell me you are having second thoughts *now?*"

"Of course not! There is no other way to save my people!" she huffed, but her eyes were filled with a sea of uncertainty.

"Of course," I agreed, and she blinked. "You could never have agreed to a water supply contract with King Cedric while working with him and Prince Sterling to find a solution. Even though Prince Sterling would have traded wishes for a cure to the plague you created, and devoted himself to saving your people had you asked, it might have been too long of a process. And it would have been too challenging for you to negotiate with Harland or Sylvaine, either. No, massacring an entire country was clearly your *only* option."

Nyra's face flushed scarlet at my mockery. "A pampered little *princess* like you could never possibly understand!"

I stared at her emotionlessly. "Cut the lies. You know my story, you know why I am slowly dying a cursed death. Why did you *really* come down here, Woman-King of dust and death?"

She balled her hands into fists. Her mouth opened and closed like a fish's, as if she were trying to refute me, but coming up with nothing. Finally, her shoulders slumped. "I do not know why I came. It is far too late to make a different choice now."

I narrowed my eyes in suspicion. Was she being serious? Or was this some sort of trick? But if she truly *was* having second thoughts, should I at least try to talk her out of it? "The things you have done are unforgivable. But...that does not mean it is too late to change course."

Nyra looked down, her long, dark hair falling over her face like a curtain. "All I wanted...was to prevent anyone else from sharing my sister's fate." Her voice was thick with emotion.

"You could still accomplish that," I said guardedly. "Our story does not have to end like this—"

Her shoulders started shaking, and for a moment, I thought she was crying. But then she threw her head back, her laughter growing in volume until it echoed throughout the dungeons. A few greasy strands of hair dangled over her eyes, which had taken on a mad gleam.

"Oh, that was good. You really do have a bleeding heart," she cackled. "The desert would have swallowed you whole."

I just sighed, leaning my head back against the rough stone and looking up at the dark ceiling. I had suspected as much, but it still felt like my heart had been twisted and squeezed, wringing the last of my emotions out of it. At least I would die knowing I had done everything that I could. I would have no regrets. I smiled.

Nyra's laughter cut off abruptly. "I have no time to waste. The ritual begins at dusk—a little earlier than planned, but a little birdie told me I would be expecting guests tonight."

My smile froze. I slowly lowered my eyes to Nyra's, knowing she was digging for a reaction, but too horrified to care. Had Adelaide been found out?!

Nyra smirked, and I had never wanted to punch someone as badly as I did now. "What...do you mean?"

"One of my lovers noticed that the black-haired witch was acting strangely, and managed to listen in on your little heart-to-heart the other night." Her grin widened, looking monstrously grotesque on her almond-shaped face. "Thanks to your paltry scheming, I will be ready to welcome the runaway prince with open arms—saving me the trouble of hunting him down. And with all of his untapped magical power, I will finally be able to revive my beloved oases."

"No," I whispered, horror choking me. What had we done? By trying to help Orion, I had only made things worse—for all of us.

Nyra flicked her long hair back and sauntered away, pausing only to say over her shoulder, "Pity you will not be around to see the grand fulfillment of my wish."

15

Orion

I t was time.

I stood under the shade of the great cedar tree my parents had planted when they first came to this land. The thin strip of forest between the back of the castle and the northern mountains was rarely frequented by anyone, but it was an integral part of my plan.

And as far as I could tell, Nyra and her thugs had not given it a second glance.

As the golden sun inched closer to the horizon, everyone was taking their places. If all went well, by this time tomorrow, the Kingdom of the Stars would no longer be under the thumb of the desert tyrant. And Astrid would be free of her curse and back in my arms.

The sun began to set, gilding the walls of the castle a brilliant gold.

"Begin." I rested my hand on the hilt of my sword, excitement and steely determination raging through me.

Beside me, Raiden raised his hands, the druids we had strategically placed in a loose perimeter around the castle undoubtedly doing the same. For a moment, nothing happened. But then an unnatural mist rose from the ground, swirling around our legs.

As the sun sank, the mist rose. Even my long, dark cloak could not completely ward off the accompanying chill. By the time dusk had settled, the misty fog hovered over the castle in a giant dome, obscuring our sight beyond a few feet in front of us. Fortunately, there was hardly any wind, so we would only need a handful of druids to keep the dome intact.

"The animals?" I asked Raiden.

Without opening his eyes, he reported, "Causing plenty of mayhem, as planned. Most of their bows and crossbows are no longer functional, and the bats and birds are keeping up a constant barrage as we speak."

"Good." I pulled out my watch and sent the starnote I had already written out.

I sensed more than saw the starships rise and sail through the air above our heads towards the castle, their hulking frames like phantom giants. I could hear an eerie clicking echoing through the mist, the sound oddly dampened, as the starship captains readied their weapons.

"Now," I said, pulling out a small glass vial, "bottoms up."

Tilting my head back, I swallowed down the bitter liquid. Nova, Castor, and Aria had been up since Adelaide's arrival, producing enough doses of sandberry antidote to give to most of our forces. Everyone also carried at least two doses of poison antidote as well. One for themselves, and one to give to a wounded comrade. Behind me, Noctus, Rigel, Rafe, and a small contingent of the most elite warriors from Sylvaine and Harland did the same.

"We await your command, Prince Sterling." Noctus bowed, the others following suit. I turned to face them.

A lump rose in my throat, but I swallowed it down. "I thank you all for your bravery. Through your actions tonight, we will save not just Astoria, but the entire continent from the threat of the Woman-King and the witches who serve her." As I spoke, I allowed a sliver of my magic to rise to the surface, turning my hair to silver and sending wisps of starlight into the air around me. I unsheathed my sword and held it aloft, the starsteel glowing with power. "Take heart, and follow me into the night—for the stars are on our side!"

The slither of steel whispered in the night, as every warrior raised his or her weapon high and chanted, "Down with the Woman-King! Long live the stars!"

A feeling of pride swelled in my chest. Not for myself, but for everything that we had accomplished together. Thanks to our common enemy, Astoria, Harland, and Sylvaine were united in one goal for the first time in living memory. It was a beautiful sight.

"Onward!" I raised my sword higher for a moment before lowering it once more.

I kept it in front of me as I plunged into the hidden underground tunnel, whose entrance had been concealed by an illusion from a wish from decades ago. The light from my sword revealed the packed earthen walls, along with the few roots that had managed to poke through them into the cool air.

A hush fell over the group as we descended into the earth, the only sound the soft patter of boots on packed dirt. Rigel and Noctus were comforting presences at my back, but I felt my senses heightening with every step.

The last time I had been in the castle, I had held my father in my arms as he took his last breath. It grated on me that I did not even know what had become of his body. Had Nyra laid him to rest, or had she simply left him out in the refuse pile with all of the others she had killed?

I gritted my teeth at the thought, holding back the sense of grief that threatened to drag me under its unrelenting waves once more. I had to be strong—too many people were counting on me. *Astrid* was counting on me. Perhaps, once this was all over, I could finally say my proper goodbyes. But until then, I would let my grief fuel my fury.

The earth shook around us, and some dust showered down on our heads. I heard a few nervous mutters behind me, so I said, "The starships have begun firing their comet cannons.

The other groups, led by Sirius, Commander Regis, and Birken, should be engaging the tribesmen at this very moment, luring them away from the castle's keep for us."

The murmuring quieted down, and the tunnel sloped steeply downward. I pushed a little more magic into my sword, increasing the radius of its glow to help everyone see. We were under the castle now, and fast approaching the danger than waited for us there.

"How long has this tunnel been here?" Rigel asked quietly.

Grateful for the distraction from my thoughts, I answered, "Since the castle was built."

I could hear the disapproving frown in his voice. "This is a huge security risk. Why did your parents keep this here?"

I smiled ruefully, ignoring the stab of pain I felt at the memory. "Sometimes, they wanted to get away from the castle and all the pomp and circumstance that came with it to spend some quality time together—alone. Sir Magnus would have insisted on sending guards with them, so this was how they snuck out. They also reasoned it could be an emergency escape route if they ever needed it."

"My father would have had a fit if he found out." I could hear an echoing sadness in his voice that matched mine.

"Could the tribesmen have used this tunnel when they invaded?" Noctus sounded worried.

"No. They used mirage magic to walk right through the front gates." I remembered the confusion of the guards on duty that night, and how they thought they had already opened the gate for me once.

"So is that how you have been sneaking out of the castle to go into town?" Rigel smiled.

I grinned. "Perhaps. Perhaps not."

We rounded a bend in the tunnel, and the path began to slope upwards, signaling we were nearing the exit.

"Be prepared to engage the enemy at any moment once we surface. Remember, their blades are coated with poison, and they may try to use mirage magic to blend into their surroundings, or even to look like an ally to deceive you. But a touch of starsteel will dispel the illusion." Rigel gave some last-minute instructions as the path began to level off.

My starlight revealed a simple wooden door with a thick starsteel lock. I took out the key, which was the spare I always kept at the guildhouse, and winced at the slight *clicking* sound when it unlocked. I paused, holding my breath as I listened for any sound of alarm from the other side of the door.

Hearing nothing, I slowly turned the handle and inched the door open. The small room on the other side of the door was a decorated sitting room, with several chairs and couches encircling a low wooden table, and several oil paintings of the night sky lining the pale blue walls. A single vase was filled with wilted flowers on the table. Only a thin beam of light from under the closed door to the rest of the castle illuminated the space, which was filled with a musty, sweet scent.

I stepped into the room to allow everyone else to filter in behind me. But as I walked past the table, the vase croaked at me. My blood froze in my veins, my senses immediately searching for traces of magic. I heard a muffled curse from a shadowy corner of the room, and then the door to the tunnel slammed shut, trapping us inside.

The mirage magic faded, stripping away the illusions. Headwitch Brunhilde lounged on the couch directly opposite me, a cage containing a black raven on the table in front of her. And lining the walls were dozens of tribesmen, their poison-coated scimitars all aimed at me.

I mentally kicked myself. There had been so much magic in the air from the druids that I had not sensed this ambush.

"What wonderful timing," croaked the old hag, her withered lips contorting into a feral grin. "How thoughtful of you to save me the trouble of hunting you down."

Noctus and Rigel drew their swords, flanking me protectively. But Rafe took a step forward, his eyes glued to the bird in the cage.

"You do not appear quite as surprised as I was expecting." I glanced at the exit, wondering if the door had been locked from the outside.

"A little birdie told me you might be coming." She ran her fingers over the bars of the bird cage, and it tried in vain to peck them. I noticed that the raven had strange, star-shaped white markings on its chest and wingtips. "Adelaide made a marvelous spy, even if she *is* useless as a witch."

Had Adelaide betrayed us *again?!* Had she somehow faked the amulet, or tricked or blackmailed Astrid into giving it away? No, that was simply not possible based on how that magic worked. Panic clawed at my throat, greedily devouring every rational thought.

The walls felt like they were closing in on me, sucking the air from my lungs. Was I about to witness everyone I had led here perish right before my eyes? All because I was entirely incapable of telling friend from foe? I began to desperately reach for my magic with the vague idea of blasting my way out of this coffin-sized room.

"Release her!" Rafe practically growled, stepping forward menacingly. His tone broke through the fear clouding my mind.

My eyes widened a fraction as I realized he was referring to the raven. And then it hit me; the white markings were caused by the corrupted starsteel bangles. Which meant the Headwitch had completely sealed off all of her magic. And if the Headwitch had done that before turning her into a bird and imprisoning her in a cage, that meant Adelaide had not willingly betrayed us.

If she had, she would have been haughtily smirking at me from that couch in her human form. And her powers would have more than likely been unsealed as a reward.

Which meant I needed to go fishing to figure out how much the hag knew.

The witch *tsked,* her lip curling when she looked at Rafe. "You were always more trouble than you were worth, mutt."

Rafe bared his teeth in a wolfish snarl. "Why did you bother keeping me alive for so long then, instead of sacrificing me like the others?"

"For my revenge," she wailed, clearly reveling in the attention. "This useless bird's mother, our foolish former Headwitch, tried to call a truce with that insipid Druid King. But your grandfather killed my daughter during what was supposed to be a routine raid. An eye for an eye, a tooth for a tooth, and a son for a daughter. But a swift death would have been too far good for you! I had originally planned to frame the last Headwitch for your gruesome demise, but she went and got herself killed by the Yellowboils first."

Adelaide let out an agonized cry. Apparently the hag had been lying to her all along. Rafe's hands balled into fists.

Before he could lunge at the revolting bag of bones and prompt the tribesmen to attack, I pulled him back and whispered, "When I give the signal, I need you to make a wish."

He nodded tersely, and the hag cackled. "Put a leash on your dog."

Without releasing my grip on his arm, I quickly asked, "Do you really think you can get away with this?"

The tribesmen were getting antsy, but I needed to buy more time so I could flesh out my plan. I just needed to keep the witch talking for a little while longer. But was she truly that oblivious, or was she monologuing for a reason?

"We already have," she gloated. "The Woman-King was unimpressed with your little rescue attempt—she knew you would use the most obvious ploys. We did have to begin the ritual a little earlier than planned, but once I add you and this," she paused, pulling out my mother's amulet and dangling it in the air tauntingly, so that the star sapphire glittered in the low light, "Everything will go according to plan." She licked her dry lips, eyeing me hungrily. "And the Redgraves will get to keep the leftovers."

My eyes snagged on the amulet. "You must be terribly confident if you dared to bring that near me."

The tribesmen muttered uneasily behind her.

The witch's eyes flicked behind me, scanning all the warriors at my back. "You might as well surrender now. You are outmatched, outclassed, and powerless to stop me." When I raised an eyebrow, she smirked. "The little birdie told me how you do not even know how to use your own magic."

I raised my glowing sword higher, and she stammered, "Except out of weak, emotional desperation."

"A good spy indeed." I reached for my magic. "Oh, and by the way, that sandberry incense you are waiting to kick in will not be working on us. Rafe, now!"

"I wish for darkness!" he shouted, lunging forward. I doused the lights, including the light from my sword. "I wish that mirage magic will no longer work in this room!"

"I wish for the door to the bird cage in front of me to be unlocked!" Three points in my back burned, but I heard a metallic squeak, followed by the furious croaking of a raven and a blood-curdling scream.

"I wish for a blinding light behind us!" Rigel yelled. I created a small star behind us, which caused all of the tribesmen to shield their eyes and cry out in pain, and Rigel and his men surged forward with a yell to engage them.

Steel rang against iron and sparks flew through the air. Two tribesmen went down, then three more. A Harlandish soldier fell, and a druid cried out in pain.

"I wish for Aaron and Cyprus to be healed of all injuries!" Noctus cried, and I grinned as I granted his wish.

The two men rose once more, their weapons raised. The tribesmen who had cut them down took a startled step back, which was all the opening my people needed.

I turned my attention back to the Headwitch, but paused at the gruesome sight before me. The raven had left nothing but a bloody mess where the hag's eyes had been. Rafe had shifted into his wolf form and had her pinned to the couch with his massive strength.

As I watched, he ripped the amulet from around her neck, the chain snapping from the force. Adelaide shifted back into her human form and snatched the blood-flecked amulet from the air as Rafe tossed it to her.

"Orion, catch!" But as the witch turned around and threw the amulet, I saw dark magic gathering around the sightless hag.

"You will pay for this, Adelaide!" Brunhilde shrieked.

"Rafe!" I cried, knowing I was too far to help.

Rafe leaped off the hag and tackled Adelaide, forcing her to the ground and out of the way of the dark magic shooting away from Brunhilde's gnarled hands. Instead of striking Adelaide, the witch's magic shattered my mother's amulet into a thousand tiny pieces.

16

Orion

A part of me shattered along with it.

Everyone went still.

The hag froze, her face going pale. "What have I done?" She fell to her knees and groped at the shards of gemstone and metal on the floor, the tiny pieces drawing blood or slipping through her gnarled fingers. Then her face contorted into a mask of twisted fury as she turned her sightless face towards Adelaide. "Look what you made me do! I should have killed *you* instead!"

With a wordless shriek, she launched herself at Adelaide and Rafe. Dark magic gathered around her claw-like hands, and Rafe surged forward to meet her with his dagger drawn.

"You will pay dearly for this!" Brunhilde waved her hand, and Rafe was sent flying into a wall. Rafe crumpled, and his dagger clattered to the floor. She advanced on Adelaide, who was struggling to rise. "Just like your mother did!"

"You always told me my mother was a disgrace to the name of Redgrave. But where *you* sought only war, *she* would have ushered in an era of peace!" Adelaide rasped. "And you betrayed your own Headwitch to take her place! You are a traitor to the coven!"

Brunhilde's face purpled. "A soft-hearted witch is no witch at all! You are just like her—a powerless failure!"

In the next instant, magic the color of rotten blood shot from Brunhilde and hit Adelaide. She let loose a blood-curdling scream as she fell back to the ground. Her body started convulsing uncontrollably, and she began to gasp for air. Her eyes went wide and her hands flew to her neck as she clawed desperately at the magic, but to no avail.

"No wonder...you always treated Helga better than me," Adelaide wheezed, glaring her defiance at the hag. "Both...untalented...and cruel."

"Adelaide!" I lunged towards her, jolted into motion by her cry of pain.

To my surprise, Noctus also made as if to help her, despite his previous distrust of her and his desire to kick her out of our group. His throwing knives flashed through the air, but dropped to the ground a few feet away from the hag, as if they had hit an invisible wall.

I tried to reach Adelaide as well, but the air shimmered in front of me, and I slammed into an invisible barrier. Cursing, I stepped back. Better to fight magic with magic.

"Noctus!"

"I wish for Brunhilde's magic to be sealed!" he said immediately.

I called on my magic and sent it straight at the wizened old hag. But instead of reaching through the barrier, as I expected, the magic came to an abrupt halt. My eyes widened in shock.

"I...I cannot break through it."

The hag threw back her head and cackled. "Did you think sealing magic was the only thing corrupted starsteel can do?!"

Did that mean it could be used to *block* star magic instead of amplify it, even without skin contact? The implications of a coven of witches immune to any and all star magic and starsteel were daunting.

Noctus cursed, and I felt like doing the same. I felt helpless as I watched Adelaide's lips start to turn blue. I needed to figure out a way to help her, and fast. For the moment, the tribesmen had paused their attack, uncertain if they should be helping the witch who had just destroyed the item Nyra needed to restore their oases, or punish her instead.

Rafe rose unsteadily and tried to stab the old hag, only for his dagger to bounce off the barrier. He shifted into his wolf form and leaped at her, fangs bared, only to be flung into a side table. He crashed into it hard, shattering the wood into splinters. He whimpered and shifted back into his human form, clutching at his side. Rafe rose and staggered over to the barrier, looking defeated, his eyes glued to Adelaide's face. He knelt down as close as he could get, and pressed his hand against the barrier.

Her eyes locked on his, and she slowly raised one trembling hand towards his. The love and desperation in his eyes as they searched hers pulled at my heart. For an instant, I imagined Astrid and I in their places.

"What are you doing, you fools?!" The hag snapped at the tribesmen. "It does not matter if the amulet is gone—so long as we have the prince, the ritual will proceed as planned. Helga is beginning as we speak, so do your duty and capture the prince!"

Spurred into motion, the tribesmen surged forward with a yell. I brought my sword up just in time to block a strike that would have severed my arm from my shoulder. Grunts echoed around me, as my forces re-engaged the rest of the tribesmen as well.

I gritted my teeth, my mind racing to find a way out of this sticky situation. I glanced at Rafe and Adelaide, whose face was losing color at an alarming rate. If I did not do something soon, we were going to lose her. A week ago, I might have been fine with that. But now...

The hiss of iron cutting through the air gave me enough warning to dodge to one side, as a scimitar cut through the space I had just occupied. Apparently, we had different definitions of *capture*.

"She said *capture*, not dismember," I muttered, half-jokingly.

The burly man grinned. "*Uninjured* was never specified."

I raised an eyebrow and rained my own series of blows down on him. He parried well, but then he started moving slower. I pushed my advantage, forcing him back a few steps towards the hag. I feinted to one side and whipped my sword up and around, slashing his sword arm. He dropped his scimitar and stumbled backwards into the barrier.

I frowned when I saw that he could not cross the magic line either. Before he could attack again, I turned my gaze back to Adelaide. Rafe was talking to her, but the young witch was struggling less and less. The sealing choker and star necklace glittered in the dim light.

I heard Rigel grunt in pain, and saw another tribesman go down. Only eight left. Steeling my resolve, I lunged forward and skewered my own opponent, who slumped to the ground at the edges of the barrier.

"Adelaide! Use the wish contained in the pendant!" I ordered, knowing this could not continue.

Her red eyes slowly drifted to me. "No... Astrid!"

"I can still save her, even without my mother's wish. So use it!" I hoped I would not come to regret using my backup plan on the witch who had once betrayed me.

But somehow, I knew this was what Astrid would have wanted.

"Use it, Adelaide!" Rafe's voice was rough, and his golden eyes were bright with emotion.

Still, Adelaide shook her head.

"You can only help Orion save Astrid if you are still alive," Rafe begged. "Besides, are you really going to let Brunhilde win? After everything she did to you? To your mother? To me?"

Adelaide closed her eyes.

"Please...you promised you would never leave me behind again!" Rafe howled desperately.

Adelaide's eyes snapped open, her eerie red eyes filled with tears. Her other hand rose to grip the star pendant, and her lips formed words I was too far away to hear.

A blinding flash lit up the room, and for an instant, I felt my mother's presence all around me. The starlight caressed my cheek with its phantom touch and connected with my own magic, energizing me and providing a sudden surge of power.

There was a sound like shattering glass, and Brunhilde screamed as her magic vanished completely.

17

Orion

The hag staggered back as the light faded, and I wasted no time. I ran her through with my sword, before yanking it out and decapitating her for good measure.

I was taking no chances.

The room went silent as the witch's body slumped to the ground a few feet from Adelaide and Rafe. The druid was now holding his witch in his arms, and I was relieved to see that the color was quickly returning to her drawn face.

A small part of me withered when I saw the pendant-less chain hanging around her neck, a glaring reminder that I had lost my mother's gift to me. Though I supposed I could consider Adelaide's life as that gift, now. Even if she could not lead me to Astrid, I would consider it a gift well-spent.

"Is she really...?" Adelaide's voice shook with emotion.

"Gone." Rafe tucked her head under his chin in a way that made me ache to do the same for Astrid. "She can never hurt us again."

"Perhaps not, but we certainly can!" A tribesman lunged towards the pair, but Noctus was there to intercept him. Rafe tugged her out of the way, putting his own body in between her and the threat.

"Take no prisoners!" I raised my sword as a yell went up from my allies, and I charged in alongside them.

After all, I had no intention of being a king who only gave orders from the safety of the rear.

I brought my sword down towards a tribesman's head with full force. When he deflected with his own scimitar, I used the momentum to arc my blade around and to the side. He grunted in pain as the starsteel bit into his shoulder, but managed to pull back before it could slice too deep. We circled each other for a moment, until he switched his scimitar to his other hand and lunged at me with a yell.

I danced to the side, and his weapon whistled through the air, where I had just been standing. I whirled and slammed my blade into his. They locked, and it became a contest of strength. My wrist ached from the strain, and my opponent grinned like a wolf stalking its prey. I grinned back and pushed him backwards. His grin disappeared.

"Not so confident now, are we?" I taunted him, refusing to let him see how much I was straining. "Those muscles just for show?"

"Bold words from a dead man," he sneered at me.

"The power of the stars will *never* be used for the sake of you desert barbarians!" I snarled. "I would rather *die* than see my starlight used for evil murderers like you!"

His face flushed scarlet. "Then I will send you back to those damned stars of yours!"

He heaved against me, breaking the lock and sending me staggering back. I pretended to lose my balance, baiting him into a forward attack. He took his chance, wearing a triumphant smirk, and gripped his scimitar in both hands to deliver a devastating overhead blow.

But I was faster.

I dropped to my knees, just as Jolene had taught me, and thrust my sword towards his exposed chest. His beady black eyes widened in shock, but it was too late. His momentum carried him onto my blade.

He stumbled and looked down at his chest in disbelief. Blood bubbled on his lips. "You are already too late."

I scowled, but before I could ask him what he meant, he keeled over, dead. I withdrew my sword, and turned to find my next opponent.

Rigel and his men looked to be handling themselves nicely, so I glanced at the other side of the room to see wolf Rafe and Noctus fighting a particularly large and bearish tribesman, who wielded a massive morningstar, which was a spiked metal ball on the end of a wooden club. The man towered over everyone here, and his unruly beard covered his broad chest almost down to his belt.

I shook my head. What did they feed these people that made them grow as big as beasts?

I stealthily approached, watching carefully for an opening I could use to end the fight. While Rafe distracted the big man by lunging at his legs and snapping his sharp fangs at his ankles, Noctus darted around to his blind spots, twin daggers drawn and ready. Several of his smaller throwing knives stuck out of the tribesman's back and sides, making him look for all the world like an overgrown porcupine.

Apparently, he had hardly even felt the knives sticking out of him, and looked more irritated than pained. No wonder those two were having such a hard time with him; it was a terrible match-up.

Rafe lunged for his ankles, and managed to sink his teeth in, thanks to Noctus' simultaneous attack on his eyes. The big man merely grunted and swatted Noctus away, as if he were some fly buzzing around him. He then turned his attention to Rafe, and raised his morningstar, readying to bash it into the wolf's side.

I could tell from the look in Rafe's golden eyes that he refused to move one inch and leave the weaponless Adelaide exposed.

"I am Rajah, the Buboloki Chieftain! I eat things like you for breakfast!" he declared with gusto. He must have been one of the chieftains Nyra had subjugated when she united the Tribes under her banner.

Before the brute could swing his morningstar like a club at Rafe's exposed side, I darted forward and plunged my sword into his broad back. It got stuck halfway. My jaw dropped as the tribesman whirled with a roar, shaking off Rafe like it was nothing. My starsword stuck out of his back, like some bizarre accessory.

He lunged at me, and I threw myself to the side, rolling to my feet to watch the charging bull nearly run straight into the opposite wall. I gaped.

Then I glanced at Noctus, my brows reaching for my hairline. He looked just as taken aback as I was.

"How is that possible?" Noctus' voice came out sounding choked.

"I think...he clenched his muscles around the blade...and squeezed until it stopped." Or at least, that was the most logical explanation I could think of.

"That is absurd," Noctus muttered. He stiffened, as the formidable man turned back towards us. "How are we supposed to take him down?"

"I have a plan. How strong is your back?"

Noctus gave me the side-eye. "That depends on what exactly you plan to have me do, Guildmaster."

I grinned. "Remember our little trip to Delphini?"

Noctus scowled. "Unfortunately."

"Good. Then get ready." I looked to Rafe, whose hackles were raised. "Can you distract him again?"

The wolf nodded.

"I will be billing you for my treatment and favorite knife once all of this is over," Noctus muttered as he handed me one of his largest throwing knives.

I took a wide stance, as the hulking tribesman barreled back towards us. "Fine, fine. You can even take two weeks off to recover."

"You have yourself a deal."

We both dove to opposite sides as the chieftain came charging in. Rafe leaped at the big man and sank his teeth into his meaty forearm. Fortunately, he had picked the one that held the morningstar.

Before he could shake the wolf off, Noctus sprinted directly behind him and bent over, angling his back like a ramp. Without hesitation, I took off running, and leaped. I used Noctus' back like a springboard and launched myself into the air above Rajah's broad back.

I reversed my grip on the knife and clutched it in two hands over my head, with the handle facing down. I had to strike just the right spot for this to work. As I reached the peak of my jump and began descending, I trained my eyes on the hilt of my sword, praying fervently that I was not about to wreck it.

I brought the back of the knife's handle down on the hilt of my sword with as much force as I could muster. With my downward momentum, I hammered my sword all the way through his chest with so much force that not even his impressive muscles could stop it.

Rajah froze, and sputtered, then looked down in disbelief to see the tip of my sword protruding from his chest. "Impossible."

He staggered, then fell, and I landed lightly beside him, panting hard. Rafe detached himself before he could be crushed under the man's weight. Somehow, we had done it!

Noctus groaned as he straightened. "I would be happy if we never had to do that again."

I clapped him on the back and he grunted. "Agreed."

I heard clapping from behind me, and turned to see that all of the other tribesmen had been finished off while we had been fighting. Rigel stepped forward and gave a low whistle.

"Impressive work!"

I glared at him. "A little help might have been nice."

"And deprive you of such great battle experience?" He shook his head. "What sort of instructor would I be if I did that?"

"A merciful one," Noctus muttered.

I laughed, some of the tension leaving my shoulders. "Yes, I would not want to describe Sir Rigel as such."

The knight laughed along good-naturedly. "Oh, and good luck getting your favorite sword back."

I groaned as I handed Noctus his knife and braced my foot against the tribesman's back to tug my starsword out of his chest. It took quite a bit more effort than I had anticipated, and I was panting by the time it was free.

After wiping the blade clean and sheathing it, I walked over to Adelaide, who was holding onto Rafe's fur like her life depended on it. The wolf let her hug him patiently, looking for all the world like any other dog—except for the spark of human intelligence in his golden eyes.

"Are you alright?" I asked as I crouched beside her.

"Yes." She nodded, but when her red eyes met mine, she burst into tears.

"Adelaide?" I reached out uncertainly, my hand hovering awkwardly in the air. Should I pat her on the shoulder in a gesture of comfort? Did witches do things like that?

"I...I want to apologize," she sniffled, and I slowly withdrew my hand.

I raised an eyebrow. That was the last thing I expected her to say.

"I am sorry for betraying you and Astrid. At the time, I thought I was doing the right thing." She gripped Rafe's fur tightly. "It took returning to my old life to realize that the things I had so desperately been chasing—my powers and my place in the coven—were no longer what I truly wanted. Or needed."

Rafe rubbed his face against hers encouragingly.

"After seeing the way the people of Astoria lived, and the kindness and protection you and Astrid offered me, I finally understood why the rest of the continent despises witches. The way I was treated...like a powerless slave, and an emotional punching bag..." She shook her head sadly. "I would rather spend the rest of my days as a powerless human with you than as a powerful witch."

Something in me shifted, reacting to the tears flowing down her cheeks. I was no druid, but even I could feel the heartbreaking sincerity in her words.

"I am sorry for using the wish you meant for Astrid." Her lower lip trembled as she met my gaze. "And I understand if you never want to see me again. Just please...let me help you save Astrid. Let me atone for bringing her here in the first place."

Without hesitating this time, I reached out and placed a hand on her shoulder. "Thank you for apologizing, and for what you risked to do the right thing."

"Can you ever forgive me?" Her ruby eyes glimmered with emotion.

I hesitated, and saw shame and devastation written across her features. Could I forgive her? Rafe flicked an ear at me, but I decided to answer honestly, "Ask me that again after we have saved Astrid."

Adelaide nodded, and straightened her spine. Determination was written in the slant of her shoulders.

"Good. Now, I want you to lead us to Astrid. But first..." I trailed off as I reached for one of my precious few bottles of liquid starlight and gestured for Noctus and Rigel to join me.

I glanced at the two men. "Hold him down."

Immediately, the knight and the former thief grabbed the wolf and pinned him to the floor before he could react.

I uncorked the bottle and dumped half over Adelaide and half over me. I put a starsteel bracelet on my wrist and pulled a starsteel gauntlet onto my right hand. I coaxed my power up to the surface, concentrating so much of it in my gauntleted hand that the metal began to glow. Starlight danced in the air around us, and I heard the others step back. Rafe went ballistic when I reached that hand towards Adelaide's neck, but I did not look away from Adelaide.

"Make your wish."

Her eyes widened, but she quickly understood what I meant. "I wish to be freed from the corrupted starsteel that is sealing my magic."

I closed my burning-hot, starsteel-covered fingers around the choker encircling her neck, and grinned when the corrupted starsteel began to sizzle.

18

Astrid

"The rebels are attacking!"

My spirits soared.

"All warriors, to arms!"

"Chief, all of the bows and crossbows are inoperable! Those damn rodents chewed through all of the strings!"

I chuckled dryly. Orion must have succeeded in allying with my aunt after all. Only he would think of having the druids command rodents to disarm his enemies before he even arrived.

"Then grab the spears, instead, you fool!"

The shouts mixed with the constant thudding of boots running on stone. It sounded like the castle had become a hive of activity. In the distance came a sound like thunder, and the wall at my back trembled. Dust drifted down from the ceiling until the quake subsided.

I wondered if Orion had managed to gain the support of Harland as well. With the backing of both Sylvaine and Harland, not to mention those who were still loyal to him here in Astoria, Prince Sterling had a real, fighting chance of stopping Nyra before it was too late.

I just hoped he was wise enough to see the trap Nyra had laid for him before he walked right into it. And that Adelaide was still alive.

My fingers automatically rose to my throat, searching for the pendant that was no longer there. I swallowed thickly as the curse pulsed, sending another bolt of agony through my body.

A little longer...

If I could just hold on a little longer...

I might get to see him one last time.

A part of me hoped that Orion had somehow, miraculously learned how to properly use his magic in the short time we had been apart. But at the same time, another part of me hoped he had not.

After all, if Orion sacrificed his life to save me from this curse, just like his mother had... The thought of living on without him was unbearable. Even if I lived, I would never be able to forgive myself. And with no heir to the throne, even if Nyra were defeated, some other tyrant was just as likely to rise in her place.

Or even worse, what if Orion failed in the attempt? He had barely survived his last encounter with the Woman-King. I bit my lip, trying to chase away such morose thoughts. I told myself that he was stronger now, that he would not make the same mistake twice.

I was so lost in my thoughts that I did not notice I was no longer alone until the door to my cell rattled. I looked up, startled to see Tariq standing on the other side of the bars. My mind raced. What was Nyra's lover doing here? Had he been ordered to kill me?

My stomach sank.

He inserted the key into the lock and opened the door. He strode towards me confidently, and I watched him warily. A week or two ago, I might have tried to escape. But now, I was too weak to even stand.

But that did not mean I had to tell *him* that.

"It is rude to enter a lady's room without permission." I paused to look him up and down. "Do they not teach manners to harem boys?"

Tariq looked down his hooked nose at me and curled his lip. He backhanded me across the face so hard that my vision went dark around the edges. I gasped, squeezing my eyes shut against the pain. It seemed my comment had hit a sore spot.

"Women in my country do not speak unless spoken to." He hauled me roughly to my feet, being none too gentle about it.

"Except for the one that gives you orders, apparently," I wheezed.

I braced for another slap. I could already feel my cheek swelling, and I would have bet a silver that it was already starting to bruise.

Instead of replying, Tariq grabbed me under the armpits and dragged me out of my cell. For a moment, my face burned with embarrassment at being hauled around like an oversized puppy.

But then I remembered I did not care what Tariq or any of his people thought of me.

I paid attention as Tariq dragged me out of the dungeons. I blinked in discomfort at the abundance of light that filled the halls from all of the lit torches, and noticed that many of the fine tapestries and gilded oil paintings were gone.

I clenched my jaw. Had the tribesmen been stripping the palace of everything of value to take with them back to the desert?

Looters and thieves, the lot of them.

It took me a moment to realize that I hardly saw any tribesmen at all. The few that I did spot were running this way and that, weapons drawn and faces set with worry. Whatever distraction tactics Orion had come up with, they were working.

So why did they need *me?*

I bit my lip. Adelaide had promised to lead Orion to me, but if Adelaide had been caught, then did that mean Nyra was simply moving me to a new location so that Orion could not find me?

Or had he already breached the castle? Was Nyra going to use me as a bargaining chip, or even as a human shield?

Tariq moved quickly through the halls and up a few flights of stairs. I stumbled trying to go up the steps, so he grunted in irritation and lifted me up higher, so that my feet dangled above the steps. He was careless, though, and my ankles hit the sharp edges a few times.

After a few more minutes, Tariq slowed to a stop in front of a pair of grand double doors. There were over two dozen tribesmen standing guard, but two opened one of the doors for Tariq without a word. He quickly slipped inside, and the door was hastily shut and bolted behind us.

Immediately, I saw the reason for the heightened security.

Nyra lounged on a golden throne in the middle of the room. An expensive carpet and dozens of pieces of furniture had been pushed against the walls on both sides of the spacious area. A massive, circular design composed of strange, unfamiliar symbols was drawn in charcoal on the marble floor. For some reason, the arcane symbols sent a shiver through me.

Helga knelt on the floor, a stick of charcoal in one hand and a bundle of sage in the other. As Tariq dragged me around the edges of the room, being careful not to step on the markings, I watched as the witch drew more odd symbols on the ground and placed a bowl filled with stardust within a charcoal circle. Now that I was looking for them, I saw dozens of similar bowls placed at regular intervals around the circle.

Nyra and her throne were positioned in the very center of the eerie design. A chill ran down my spine. Was this the ritual

Adelaide had spoken of, that would tie every Astorian's lifeforce to Nyra's?

But why was Helga the one working on this? I would have expected Headwitch Brunhilde to be the one in charge of the ritual. Where was she?

Without warning, Tariq threw me down at Nyra's feet, within the borders of the central circle on the floor. He muttered complaints about me under his breath as he took up position beside his lover, though he took care not to step on the charcoal lines. The rest of her harem stood either behind her throne or along the edges of the room.

I slowly raised my gaze to hers as I settled into a seated position. She sneered down at me, raking her dark eyes over my thin frame and tattered dress. But despite her calm veneer, I could tell she was on edge. She was nervous.

Good.

My lips lifted into a slight smile, and Nyra frowned. "I would hazard a guess that Orion and his allies are putting up more of a fight than you anticipated."

She raised a hand to stop Tariq from brandishing his weapon at me. "His resistance is futile."

I scanned her quickly, noticing that the amulet she had worn so brazenly when she came to visit my cell was nowhere to be seen. Hope soared in my chest. Did that mean Adelaide had succeeded in stealing the amulet back from her, after all? Was that why she seemed so nervous?

"Where is the amulet?" I looked her up and down, and raised my eyebrow.

Her lips thinned. "It is safe."

"Then why do you look so nervous? So afraid?" I taunted. "Has something gone wrong?"

I knew it was unwise to rile her up, at least if I were only concerned about my own well-being. But she seemed off, and if I could rattle her further, or cause her to make a mistake, that might be all the opening Orion needed to end this nightmare.

"Everything is going according to plan," she said tightly. "*You* are the one who should be afraid."

Her nails drummed a quick rhythm against the throne's armrest. I saw Tariq glance at her out of the corner of his eye. So she was lying.

"Except I am not. So why am I here?" I pushed.

Her lips twisted into a cruel smile. "You are here as leverage—just in case. And if I do not need to use your body, then I will use your lifeforce—however weak and paltry it may be—as fuel to grant my wish. Just like all the rest of the northern heathens."

My palms went cold and clammy. I reached for the calm, numb acceptance I had been relying on so heavily since the night this southern monster forced me to choose between myself and my prince. I refused to give her the satisfaction of seeing me tremble.

Instead, I curled my lip. "Coward."

This time, she did not stop Tariq from hauling me to my feet and pressing the edge of his blade to my neck. The sickening scent of the poison he coated the metal with scraped at my nostrils. One cut from that blade and my lifespan would be measured in breaths. My heart pounded in my chest at the memories that horrid odor conjured.

"How dare you speak to her like that!" he snarled, spittle flying.

I plastered a serene smile on my face. Tariq flushed angrily, and I heard Nyra's fingers drum faster, tapping out an anxious staccato rhythm.

They needed me alive. So no matter how much scimitar-waving and posturing they did, it was all empty threats. Tariq's expression darkened, and I could tell he was a man who was used to immediate obedience. Even Nyra's other lovers seemed to fear and obey him.

I only had to be brave for a little while longer. As the curse throbbed alongside my heartbeat, sapping my strength, I could tell that I had very little time left.

"Ignore the halfling," Nyra finally rasped, and turned her attention to the witch scurrying about on the floor. "Helga! Begin the ritual at once!"

The girl startled, looking up from her work, and Tariq removed the blade from my throat. "Now? But the Headwitch still has not returned with the amulet—"

"You would dare disobey your commissioner?!" Nyra's words sliced through the air, as sharp as a whip.

"N-no, of course not, Your Majesty," Helga stammered, her eyes darting towards the door, as if hoping her mentor would suddenly appear. "I simply worry that my powers alone will not be sufficient for a grand hex such as this—"

"Begin. Now." Nyra looked down her nose at the witch. "Your warty master should be joining us shortly."

Was I imagining things, or did Nyra smirk when she said that last part? What, exactly, had Nyra ordered the Headwitch to do?

Helga's expression darkened at the clear insult, but she dutifully bowed her head, made a few final marks with her charcoal, and placed her hands palms-down, inside of two smaller circles that seemed to have been designed for that purpose.

At a gesture from Nyra, Tariq hurriedly dragged me out of the circle and to the edge of the room. The other tribesmen did the same, taking obvious care not to touch the symbols.

She began to chant, a low, eerie noise that rasped out from the back of her throat. As the witch began to sway, magic the color of burnt meat gathered in the air around her. Almost immediately, the grotesque magic was sucked into the massive circular symbol on the ground.

And then it began to glow blood-red.

I silently prayed to whatever stars were listening, that Orion would either make it here in time to stop this cursed ritual, or else that he could flee beyond its reach.

Because I could feel in my bones that Astoria would never recover from this ritual should it succeed.

19

Orion

The dungeon guard slumped to the ground at Rigel's boots. A quick search of his person revealed his key ring, and it took less than a minute to find the key that fit.

I focused my magic, using it to reach out and sense if other magic users were nearby. The castle had been unnervingly devoid of guards and tribesmen, which meant either our diversions were working, or Nyra had gathered them all elsewhere for some unknown reason.

But my magic found no one near.

Wait, no one?

The dungeon door clicked open, and I rushed inside, with Rigel and the others hurrying to keep up. I sprinted down a short hallway that slanted down, with only a few torches to light the way. I rounded the corner and stopped dead at the sight of a single isolated cell. A pile of straw took up one corner, with a chamber pot in the other.

But it was empty.

"Adelaide?"

The witch rushed forward, but stopped when she saw the empty cell. Her face paled. "She was here, I swear by the stars! This is where they kept her!"

Had this all been one elaborate trap? Had I been a fool to trust a witch who had already betrayed me once? The possibility that Astrid was already gone, in a place I could never reach her, set off a wild maelstrom of emotions in my chest, and I struggled to draw breath. I set my hand on my sword, wrestling with myself, as I slowly pivoted to face the witch.

But she was not looking at me, or even summoning her newly-unsealed magic. Instead, Adelaide entered the cell through the slightly ajar door, and crouched near the center of the back wall. Slowly, she picked up a scrap of gauzy teal fabric and held it up to me like an offering.

My eyes narrowed. There was no doubt in my mind that that was a piece of the beautifully impractical dress that Captain Jolene had given Astrid, the one she had worn to the Druidlands.

"Nyra must have moved her within the last day, since I was captured." Adelaide's eyes never left mine, begging me to believe her. Her expression was open and unguarded, her worry and fear plain on her features.

I nodded tersely, letting my hand fall to my side and away from my weapon. The sudden icy fear that had gripped me eased a fraction.

"She must have known I would lead you here if I could," Adelaide muttered, almost to herself. "But I was captured, so why..." Then her eyes went wide. "Nyra must have assumed you already knew where Astrid was being held prisoner, and moved her somewhere else. But where?"

Rigel cursed. "We do not have time to search the entire castle. She could be anywhere!"

But Noctus shook his head. "No, Nyra would not keep her just anywhere. She knows what Astrid means to Orion. She would keep her close, to use as leverage if it came to that."

"So to find Astrid, we find Nyra." I groaned internally. "But that hardly narrows it down."

"Nyra should be in the throne room, where the ritual circle was being drawn." Adelaide stood, her hand clenching into a fist around the fabric. "Unless they have redone it, of course."

"Or unless she is out commanding her warriors in one of the skirmishes outside," Rigel pointed out. "For all we know, neither of them is even within the castle."

"I can find her for you." Rafe stepped forward, a steely look in his golden eyes.

Before I could ask how, the druid had shifted into his wolf form. He padded up to Adelaide and sniffed at the scrap of fabric she still held. After just a few seconds, he turned back towards the door and put his nose to the ground, sniffing the stones like a bloodhound on the hunt.

Rafe gave a sharp bark and began moving quickly. Hope and heady anticipation replaced my fear as I hurried to follow him back out of the dungeons. The wolf's claws clicked on the bare stone as he led us down a series of hallways.

He paused for a minute at an intersection of hallways, but soon followed his nose to the base of a narrow set of servants' stairs. Rafe bounded awkwardly up the steps, taking them two at a time, and we hurried to keep up.

But as we reached the first landing, Rafe froze. He raised his hackles and bared his fangs, emitting a low growl from deep in his chest. I joined him on the landing, prepared to see a group of tribesmen bearing down on us, but there was not a soul in sight. Rigel and the others looked as confused as I felt.

And then, I felt it too.

Malevolent magic, more powerful than anything I had ever encountered, thrummed through the air. Goosebumps rose on my arms, and primal, instinctual fear chilled me to the bone.

"What is it?" Rigel asked guardedly, looking around for a threat only magic-wielders could sense.

Adelaide gasped. "Helga has begun the ritual! We must stop her before she completes it, or all of our lives will be bound to Nyra's!"

"But the amulet was destroyed! She has no way of using that lifeforce to grant her wish!" Horror rooted me to the spot.

This was the worst case scenario. It felt like the lives of all of my subjects were pressing down on my shoulders with the weight of a mountain.

"But does *she* know that?" Noctus asked grimly. "I doubt she anticipated Brunhilde would destroy it."

I rounded on Adelaide. "What happens if Helga cannot channel all of that magic power alone?"

The witch went pale. "If she successfully connects to the lifeforce of every person in range, there would be enough power there to level the castle and everything within a fifty-mile radius."

Rigel swore, and I nearly did the same.

"Can we stop the ritual once it has already begun?" Noctus' voice was strained.

"I...I am not sure," Adelaide stammered. "If we can stop her before she connects to everyone's lifeforce, then we should be able to. If not...then all of that magic will run wild."

Rigel whipped out his starwatch and quickly sent out a message. "I am calling in everyone we can spare."

"Rafe! Lead us to them!" I ordered.

He nodded once and put his nose back to the ground, and we resumed our ascent up the stairs. If we were, in fact, headed to the throne room, then we would reach it within minutes.

I let my icy rage settle around my shoulders like a cloak. I held the hilt of my starsword in a white-knuckled grip, preparing myself for the fight ahead.

This time, I would not be fooled by a mirage.

I would not be swayed by the sickly-sweet scent of sandberries.

And I would not hesitate to avenge my father.

We leaped onto the final landing, and Rafe raced ahead down the hall, straight towards the dozens of elite warriors who guarded the door.

I drew my sword, calling forth my magic and letting it spill over. The time for caution was over. Either we succeeded now, or the Kingdom of the Stars would fall forever.

I refused to fail a second time.

"We must push through!" I called, raising my sword as I charged. My breath scraped in my throat and time seemed to slow. The slither of steel filled the air around me as my brothers in arms drew their weapons.

"Knights of the Evening Star! Protect your king, and carve a path through the invaders!" Sir Rigel's voice boomed behind me, and the men answered with a wordless yell as they charged.

The tribesmen looked unsurprised to see us, and readied their weapons to meet us. Bile rose in my throat at the sight of the iridescent green sheen coating each blade, and I gritted my teeth. Tonight, those cowards would get to taste my starsteel, and see how a real warrior fights with honor.

Unease whispered through me when I did not see Tariq among them. Either Nyra was not here, or he was inside the throne room with her. Which meant I would need to save most of my magic for what lay ahead.

Rafe reached them first. He launched himself into the air and sank his teeth into the throat of an enemy. His momentum brought them both crashing down, and after a short struggle, the tribesman lay still.

Crimson magic shot like an arrow into another one, sending him to his knees. Another bolt of magic expanded into a shield around Rafe just in time to protect him from the bite of an iron scimitar. The weapon bounced off the shield and lodged in the wall.

I finally reached the tribesman who stood in front of the double doors, glaring at me. Unlike most of the others, he bore a massive battle axe in his muscled forearms.

As fast as lightning, I thrust straight for his heart. He brought his guard up just in time, the impact jarring my sword arm and numbing my hand for a few precious seconds.

"You will never get past me," he scoffed. "Not unless you are in chains!"

"You are a fool for standing between me and all I hold dear!"

The man's face twisted into a scowl, but I swung my sword around at his side before he could reply. *I did not have time for this!* I could feel the level of malicious magic in the air growing heavier by the moment. He blocked, so I spun in the opposite direction to strike his other arm. He grunted in pain as my blade bit into his skin, and I saw his form flicker for an instant before I tugged the starsword free.

I smirked. "I see someone is rather insecure about his short stature."

The taunt worked, and his face became a mask of rage. Now that I knew he was a good head shorter than he appeared, I knew exactly where to aim. I rained blows down on him, forcing him to take a step back, and then another, until his back hit the wooden doors.

I sliced at his head, but he ducked at the last second, and my blade whistled through empty air. I cursed under my breath and dodged to the side as he swung his axe at my torso. He may have been short, but he was certainly strong.

I saw a spear bearing down on me and dropped to the floor just in time.

"You have to get through, Your Highness!" Sir Rigel said as appeared to confront the spearman. "Leave them to us and go!"

I glanced around, taking stock of the battle. Noctus and Rigel were engaging two tribesmen each, as were many of Rigel's knights. Rafe was weaving through the battlefield, helping where he could, and Adelaide was doing her best to attack from a distance without accidentally hitting any of her allies.

I scowled. Rigel was right, but with everyone packed in front of the doors like this, I would likely be stabbed in the back if I attempted to open the doors now.

At this rate, we would be too late.

"For Astoria!" The ringing cry echoed through the hall. "And for our rightful king!"

I risked a glance to the side, and saw a group of knights and soldiers charging into the fray, with Sirius leading them. They took the nearest tribesmen by surprise, like a sudden tidal wave.

A few of the tribesmen hesitated, turning to face this new threat, and I felt the tide of battle shift.

"Our reinforcements have arrived!" Rigel trumpeted, and I grinned.

The distraction almost cost me, and I had to throw myself to the side to avoid being felled like a tree trunk. But the tribesman had put too much power into that swing and now stood off-balance. Taking my chance, I lunged forward and dealt him a mortal blow straight to the heart.

He staggered back against the door, a look of disbelief on his face as his mirage sputtered and went out. My heart shuddered as the terrible magic on the other side of the door ballooned, telling me I had only moments to act.

"Orion!" Adelaide screamed, the warning clear in her tone.

I pushed on the door. It did not budge.

It was bolted from the inside.

"Rigel!"

The knight danced closer to me, glanced at the door, and quickly whispered, "I wish for the doors closest to me to be unlocked and weakened."

I granted his wish.

But the brute I had just defeated was blocking them, and I did not have time to move him out of the way. So I took a few steps back, sucked in a deep breath, and charged straight ahead. Once I was a few strides away, I leaped, and drop-kicked the tribesman in the chest.

The doors burst open with a loud *bang*. I rolled to my feet in one fluid motion and drew my sword, readying my magic for the final battle.

Helga knelt at the edge of the ritual circle, half of which glowed a disturbing shade of red. Nyra lounged on my father's throne in the very center of it, and her personal harem of warriors stood against the walls, weapons already drawn.

And then my eyes snagged on Tariq. He was standing off to one side, holding a blade to Astrid's throat.

"Hello Orion darling," Nyra purred. "Take one more step, and Astrid dies."

20

Astrid

Orion froze, and slowly sheathed his sword.

Nyra smirked.

I caught a glimpse of Noctus and Sir Rigel fighting the tribesmen just beyond the door, and I felt my spirits lift. They sank when I realized that meant Orion was now facing Nyra and her elite warriors alone, and with a handicap—me. I scanned the room, mentally tallying his odds of beating so many alone.

They were not good.

I glanced at Helga, who was still intensely concentrating on chanting and channeling power into the circle. More than half of it was lit up with a blood-red glow, and I could practically hear the phantom sound of a ticking clock. Once that thing was fully charged, our time would be up.

I could practically see the gears turning in Orion's mind. He needed to stall long enough to come up with a plan to get out of this abysmal situation.

Orion glanced at me, his blue eyes softening. My lower lip quivered at the sight of him—a little battered around the edges, but most definitely alive and kicking. I tried to take a step forward, only for Tariq to tighten his grip on my arm.

"Stay still if you wish to live a little longer," he whispered against the shell of my ear. I suppressed a shudder at the sensation, and Orion's gaze hardened.

The prince returned his gaze to Nyra. "I see you have become exactly that which you despise most: a killer, a destroyer of peoples. Just like the man who doomed your sister to an early grave, along with the rest of the Tribelands."

Nyra flinched, and hurt flashed in her dark eyes. It was gone so quickly I could not be certain I had seen it at all. Then her expression darkened, and she flicked a hand at the closest warrior.

Immediately, the burly man threw four small balls around the room. Orion's brows pinched together, and he instinctively set his hand on the hilt of his sword, causing Tariq to tense.

For a few seconds, nothing happened. And then with a hiss, they released a plume of mist into the air. For a moment, I panicked, thinking they had just doomed us all by releasing their poison into the air. But when Orion's hand swung limply to his side and his expression slackened, I realized with dawning horror that Nyra had just suffused the air with copious amounts of sandberry perfume.

As the first hint of its sickly-sweet scent teased my nose, I held my breath and strategically maneuvered the loose neckline of my dress over my mouth and nose.

"Now, why not take a deep, calming breath, and we can discuss this, ruler to ruler," Nyra purred, grinning like a cat with a mouse.

I watched in horror as Orion took a deep breath, and a goofy smile bloomed on his face. Tariq relaxed his grip on me, and sheathed the dagger he had been holding against my throat.

"Nyra, what you are doing...is wrong." Orion's voice sounded slurred, as if he had drunk a pint of ale at Ace's tavern.

"Are you sure? Is it so wrong to save the lives of my people?" Nyra's voice dripped with false honey.

"I... To save your people?" Orion blinked lazily, and took a step towards Nyra.

"Yes, darling. Just like you, I want what is best for those who live in the Tribelands." Her grin widened as he moved a few steps deeper into the circle.

My heart sank. No, no, no! At this rate, Nyra would finish the ritual and then use Orion to grant her wish—most likely killing him in the process! Orion could not fall here—not like this!

"Orion, snap out of it!" I shrieked, before Tariq clamped a rough hand over my mouth.

Orion slowly turned to look at me, but his vacant expression gutted me. "Everything will be...fine, Astrid."

Orion slowly blinked one eye. I stilled. Did he just *wink* at me? I teared up before drooping in Tariq's arms, and looked at the floor to hide my stunned expression.

My mind raced. What did that mean? How was Orion not affected by the sandberries? Even I was starting to feel rather woozy and light-headed, and I had been nowhere near the sandberry bombs. The mischievous, grinning face of a certain redhead rose up in my mind's eye, and everything suddenly clicked into place.

Nova! And Castor! Had my brave apprentices returned and perfected the sandberry antidote I had been working on? If they had, and had then gone on to make big batches of it for Orion and his forces...then this was all just an act!

I carefully schooled my features into a mask of sadness and fear before I raised my face once more. Orion now stood in front of Nyra, in the middle of the circle, which was now seventy-percent charged with magic. Sweat poured down Helga's face from the exertion, and I felt a vague hope that she might run out of magic before she could fully charge it. At least she had slowed down.

"Yes, stand by my side, Orion. You may have the privilege of helping me create a new and better world for my people." Nyra gripped Orion's face, her nails digging into his skin.

But Orion did not wince.

"Will there be peace?" His voice sounded as innocent as a child's, but still, Nyra frowned.

She quickly smoothed her expression. "Of course. Everyone will be at peace."

"Everyone will be happy?" Orion pressed dreamily, and leaned closer to Nyra.

No one else seemed to notice the shiver in the air as a small form flew through the cracked door and silently approached Helga. I noticed that the sounds of fighting had begun to die down. I prayed with everything in me that it was the tribesmen and not my guildmates who had been silenced.

By the stars, I hoped that they had all been given the sandberry antidote as well, or we were in big trouble.

"Yes, they will be happy," Nyra snapped, clearly annoyed. She moved Orion so that he stood next to her throne—his throne—and glanced sharply at the circle. "Hurry it up, witch!"

I felt some of the tension in Tariq's body ease as his attention switched to Helga. This time, I held still. When the time came, I needed to be ready to do my part.

"Where is that unsightly headwitch?" Nyra muttered, before turning to Orion, as if she had only just realized she was missing. "Did you kill her? Do you have the amulet?"

Orion tilted his head as if thinking. "The one that greeted us?"

I could practically hear Nyra grinding her teeth from here. "Yes. That one."

"I killed her."

Helga stumbled in her chanting, and Nyra's gaze cut to Orion. "What?! What about the amulet?"

"I took it back." Orion shrugged, his placid smile firmly in place. "Do you want to see it?"

"Yes!" Nyra exclaimed, visibly shaken now that she was down to only one witch. "Give it to me!"

"As you *wish*," Orion said, and reached towards a small satchel on his belt, right next to his sword.

I tried not to tense when I heard the way he emphasized the word *wish*. Things were about to get exciting. And weakened or not, I had no intention of being Orion's weakness any longer.

So when Orion slapped Adelaide's corrupted starsteel magic-sealing bracelets on Nyra's wrists, I was ready. Before Tariq could react, I mustered every ounce of strength I had left and smashed the back of my head into his face.

I heard a sickening crunch, and then Tariq released me, cursing and clutching at his face. Blood poured out from between his hands, and I realized I had actually broken his nose.

I staggered a few steps away from him, before my strength abandoned me and my legs gave out. I sank to the floor as darkness licked at the edges of my vision and the curse pulsed, sending waves of agony through me. But I clung to consciousness with a fierce determination as I watched the ensuing chaos unfold.

Nyra's face twisted into a mask of pure hatred. "Kill her! Kill them all!"

Despite the fact that he could hardly see, Tariq unsheathed his scimitar and raised it high overhead, preparing to strike me

down. I braced for the blow, knowing I was too weak to even
dodge.

"Rigel!" There was a desperate edge to Orion's voice that I
had only heard once before; the day that Khalifon had nearly
taken both of our lives.

And then suddenly Sir Rigel was standing protectively
over me, his sword braced in both hands to stop Tariq's
powerful downward swing. Sparks flew as the two blades
met, and Sir Rigel grunted from the effort.

"Good to see you again, Astrid. Or should I say, *princess?*"
he quipped, as I exhaled in relief.

"It is good to see you, too." My laugh quickly devolved
into a cough.

"As for you, Tariq," Sir Rigel gritted out as he pushed him
back, away from me, "I am going to make you rue the day
you slayed my father."

Tariq managed a pained sneer. "What, was he some guard
around here?"

"He was His Majesty's Knight Protector," Sir Rigel
growled. "And had you faced him in an *honorable* duel,
instead of ambushing him with poison, it would have been
you lying on the floor that night!"

They exchanged a flurry of blows, and Tariq made a show
of trying to remember. "Are you the son of the grizzled old
fool who stood dozing outside the former king's study?"

A muscle feathered in Sir Rigel's jaw as the knight parried the tribesman's subsequent blows. "I am the son of Sir Magnus, the greatest Knight Commander this continent has ever known!"

"Ha!" Tariq scoffed. "We shall see about that!"

I could tell Sir Rigel was furious, but fortunately, he seemed to be letting his anger and need for vengeance fuel him, instead of letting it control him. Tariq scowled when he realized his taunts had not caused the knight to lose his composure, and that he was instead forcing him back, out of the circle and towards the wall. I was relieved to see that the sandberry scent had no effect on Sir Rigel, and that he was taking great care not to allow his opponent to so much as nick him with his poisoned scimitar.

Dozens of Astorian knights, as well as some druid warriors and soldiers dressed in Harlandish garb came pouring into the room, and quickly engaged the elite warriors stationed there, before they could move to obey their lover's command to kill me or anyone else.

The glowing red light from the markings on the floor began to flicker, and I looked over to see a furious raven diving and pecking at Helga. Blood coated her talons and beak, but the other witch refused to cease chanting or lift her hands from the circle. She stuttered as the raven took chunks of her stringy hair from her scalp, and faltered when the wolf slunk into the room as well and began to circle her, fangs bared and a rumbling growl emanating from his chest.

I tried to rise from my position on the floor, but a sudden wave of searing agony stole my breath, and it was all I could do to brace my hands against the floor and try to breathe through the pain. Internally, I cursed the timing of this ridiculous pain. Shudders wracked my body, as the darkness licked ever more hungrily at the edges of my vision.

I hated how powerless I felt. I should be fighting by everyone's side, not fighting for my life on the floor as a liability. This was my *home*. These were my *people*. And I wanted to fight for *them* just as fiercely as they were fighting for *me*.

If only I had my bow, or even my daggers.

If only I were free from this curse.

If only I had more time.

More strength.

I struggled to lift my gaze from the floor. Nyra had finally climbed down from her stolen throne to face Orion. Tonight, he looked every bit the prince: he was dressed in black and silver from head to toe, and his black cloak billowed out behind him in an ethereal wind. His hair and eyes glowed that heavenly silver, and even his sword seemed to glow with starlight.

The pair circled each other, Nyra with her iron scimitar and Orion with his starsword. Her dark onyx hair was pulled back in a high ponytail, and it swished behind her with every step she took. Her steps were light and measured, but her dark eyes kept glancing towards where Tariq fought with Sir Rigel.

My mind flashed back to the night when everything had begun to go wrong. Even with the thing she needed most in front of her, for both herself and her people, she had dropped everything to run to Tariq when he had fallen last time.

Without experience and through sheer force of will, she had wielded the star sapphire amulet, using its unruly magic to heal his wounds and save his life. She had turned her back on her opponent to do so.

It struck me then: despite everything that snake of a woman had done, she truly loved Tariq. Among her whole harem, he was always right by her side.

How could she possibly know what it was to love like that, and still insist on wrenching that same sort of love away from others? From me?

Or was that why she had seemed so rattled earlier?

The hint of an idea took shape in the back of my mind, taunting me with a way to see Orion through to the other side of this battle—if only I had the strength to carry it out.

But how?

Sir Rigel had already moved away from where I lay, most likely so Tariq could not blackmail him with me and so that he would have ample space to maneuver without tripping. I looked around at the other combatants, searching for a familiar face.

I saw Sirius fighting two opponents in one corner, Birken firing off spears of ice in another. Both were too far away for me to reach, and I refused to distract them at a critical moment by calling out to them.

And then I saw a familiar figure cloaked in shadows, making his way towards me through the melee. Noctus slipped through groups of fighters, delivering a fatal slash here and a well-timed strike there. When he spotted a Harlandish soldier being pushed back, he threw one of his knives into the opposing tribesman's throat. Then he continued on, as if he were taking a stroll through a field of starflowers on a cool autumn's night.

I grinned when he crouched beside me and pressed a vial of green liquid against my lips.

"Drink. Your apprentices finished your sandberry antidote." He whirled and downed another tribesman, who had been trying to sneak up on him from behind. The coward died with a startled cry.

Warmth bloomed in my chest, not from the bitter concoction, but from the thought of my two rambunctious apprentices continuing my work. Only a few moments after I had downed the whole thing, some of the fog in my mind began to burn away.

"Better?" Noctus asked gruffly.

"Better." I handed back the vial, and he held my hand for a beat longer than necessary. His dark eyes expressed to me what his words could not. I had missed him, as well.

"Take this, too." He passed over a vial of liquid starlight, but when I hesitated to take it, he gently wrapped my cold fingers around it.

"Orion might need this," I protested weakly, though my eyes were glued to the mesmerizing liquid as it glittered and swirled within the glass. My mouth watered, my body screaming out for me to take it to make the pain go away.

"That is why I brought a whole satchel of extras." Noctus pushed the vial towards my lips. "So quit arguing and drink it already."

I tipped my head back and downed the whole thing in one go. Ace would have been beaming with pride if he had seen me do that in his tavern. A welcome coolness spread from my stomach outward, dulling the waves of agony and beating back the darkness that threatened to consume me. I sighed in relief as my headache receded, and I could finally think more clearly.

"Thanks." The ghost of a smile curved my cracked lips. "Now, please tell me you brought my daggers or my bow with you."

Noctus gave me the grin that normally made those he interrogated shudder in fear. "But of course."

I matched his grin when I felt the familiar woodgrain of my bow in my hands once more, and turned my sights on the enemy.

21

Orion

I half-glanced at Rigel, even as I circled Nyra, relieved that he seemed to have Tariq on the defensive. Without her right-hand man, Nyra would have fewer options, and fewer chances to play her devious tricks on us.

"It would appear you did not learn your lesson last time." Nyra's scimitar whistled through the air towards my throat.

I easily blocked the strike, and she looked surprised. "Last time, I was unaware of your cowardly tactics." I delivered a few probing strikes, which she easily evaded or parried. "That is no longer the case."

Nyra scowled, and resumed circling, occasionally probing for weakness.

"Nothing to say?" I taunted her. "Are you afraid you cannot beat me without some underhanded trick or poison?"

She scoffed. "It is hardly *my* fault you refuse to use anything besides your muscles and a lump of steel to win your battles."

I fought back the rising tide of my anger. Rather than explain to this snake of a woman *exactly* how I would be defeating her, I simply grinned instead. Her eyebrows pinched together, confused by my reaction.

Lunging forward, I chopped my sword towards her waist, and when she moved to block, I reversed course and swung at her head, instead. She dropped to the floor and rolled before popping right back up.

She fought more like Captain Jolene than any trained knight or soldier. It had not occurred to me before, but she had likely been forbidden from learning the sword, just as every woman of the tribes was forbidden to learn any sort of fighting or even self-defense. Which meant she had learned primarily by watching—and after that, from her harem of warriors.

But without her mirage magic, Nyra would have to rely more heavily on her scimitar, her tricks, and her poison.

"How did you resist the scent of the sandberries?" Her dark eyes were cold, calculating.

How had I ever thought they were warm and mesmerizing? "You are not the only one on the continent who has access to information on plants."

Her eyes narrowed, and flicked to Astrid. "She made an antidote?! In such a short span of time?"

I thrust my glowing sword towards her heart, forcing her attention back to me. "You underestimated who you were dealing with."

She bared her teeth in an animalistic snarl. "A mistake I will not make again!"

"No, you will not. Because I will never give you that chance again!"

I feinted to one side before striking at the other. She barely managed to bring up her guard in time to block, and sparks flew as our blades clashed. The force of the blow sent a jarring shock up my arm. She had been training hard since the last time we crossed blades.

But so had I.

I shoved her back, and I noticed that she danced backwards, in such a way that she avoided smearing the symbols on the floor. I purposefully slid my foot across a charcoal line while watching Helga out of the corner of my eye. The witch stuttered as the ominous red light flickered.

We either needed to kill Helga or damage the circle so badly that the ritual could not proceed. Hopefully, the gathered magic would either turn on its caster or dissipate, like mist on a sunny morning.

If it did not...well, I supposed I would be finding out whether or not all that magical training had paid off.

Adelaide and Rafe seemed to be having trouble getting close to her hands, as the volatile magic Helga was channeling kept repelling them. The mounting magical pressure in the room felt like the inside of a teakettle being brought to a boil, as the magic circle neared eighty percent charged.

A flash of metal warned me just in time, and I dodged to one side as Nyra's scimitar cleaved the air where I had just been standing. She whipped her weapon around, its keen edge missing my arm by a hair.

I flinched, my body instinctively recoiling from the memory of the agony I had felt the last time she cut my arm with her poisoned blade. I needed to trust that my allies would do their part and focus the entirety of my attention on this fight.

Nyra's lips curled upward at my reaction, reminding me of a snake spotting a wounded hare. "One nick, and it will all be over for you. And unlike last time, there will be no escape."

She stepped back, giving me time to recover, instead of pressing her advantage. I frowned. Why was she hesitating? I watched as she glanced at Tariq and then Helga before licking her lips nervously.

And then it clicked. I grinned, and shuffled through more of the charcoal lines. Nyra had no intention of killing me—at least, not until she got what she wanted.

I scoffed. "Good luck restoring the oases without me *or* the amulet."

She pursed her lips, and I could tell I had hit the nail on the head. Though she needed to keep me alive, I knew she would have no qualms about injuring me, poisoning me, or blackmailing me with the lives of my friends and allies.

Still, a tiny part of me wondered if I would be able to kill her. Even after everything she had done, at her very core, she was a scared girl who was desperate to save her people—a feeling I understood all too well.

"I might spare *you,* but Astrid and the others will need to go." Nyra's dark eyes never left mine, and I could tell she meant it.

I clenched my jaw against the anger and the memories her threats revived in my mind and heart.

"Now that the amulet is gone, do you regret killing my father in cold blood?" I refused to fall for her obvious attempt to rile me up.

I anticipated what she would say, but it still hurt to hear her say it. "So long as I have you, it will all be worth it."

"Would your sister say the same?" I needed to keep her talking, keep her distracted.

"You have no right to speak of my sister!" Nyra jumped forward and brought her weapon down in a vicious overhead strike.

"I have *every* right!" I snarled, dodging to the right and returning her strike with one of my own. "It was because of *her* that you have killed hundreds of innocents!"

Memories of late nights spent in front of the fire with my father rose up in my mind, reminding me of what this woman had stolen from me. She had stolen the chance for me to hear his warm laughter, to see his eyes crinkled with worry, to feel his calloused hands on my shoulder.

My anger bubbled up from beneath the grief that had smothered it for so long. Fury was a living thing in my veins, urging me to surrender completely to my desire for vengeance.

Instead of refuting me, Nyra gave a wordless yell as she rained down a flurry of blows. I parried every single one, determined to uphold my promise to myself so that I would not find myself in the same position as the last time we had fought—poisoned and defeated.

The time for taunting and distraction was over. The real battle had finally begun.

When Nyra swung for my legs, I surprised her by jumping up and landing on the flat of the blade—pinning her in place. Her eyes went wide as my blade cut into her arm, but she released her scimitar and twisted in place to quickly dislodge my blade before it could bite too deep.

She yanked on her scimitar with her good arm, and I stepped back as she pulled a second time, so that she and her weapon went stumbling back. Nyra knocked over a bowl filled with liquid starlight, and cursed as it slowly rose into the air. A portion of the nearby glowing markings went dark.

She cursed again. I grinned.

"You should be honored to give your life for the greater good," Nyra hissed as she leveled her scimitar at me.

I scoffed. "Whose greater good? *Yours?*"

"Precisely!"

This time, she swung at my head, so I ducked low and swiped at her legs. She jumped back and twirled away from my follow-up strike. She yanked at the cuffs on her wrists in an attempt to release the corrupted starsteel binding her, but to no effect.

My foot nudged something, and I glanced down to see another bowl of liquid starlight. Seeing that I was distracted, Nyra charged. I quickly bent down, grabbed the bowl, and threw its contents into her face.

Nyra screeched as the liquid stung her eyes, blinding her temporarily. She waved her scimitar around her in a wild arc, in a clumsy attempt to keep me away while she could not see.

"Dirty tricks," she protested.

"I learned from the best pirate captain there is."

I darted to the side as she chopped at the spot where she had heard my voice, so I circled around behind her. I pressed the tip of my blade right between her shoulder blades. She froze.

"Surrender," I ordered, trying to keep my voice level. If she refused, did I have it in me to run her through?

She half-turned her head, cracking one eye open. "Never."

"Orion! Behind you!" Rigel yelled.

I threw myself to the side just before Tariq's scimitar cleaved the air where I had just been standing. Rolling to my feet, I saw that the tribesman had broken free from Rigel when he had seen his lover on the verge of defeat. Rigel was sprinting towards us, a look of pure fury on his normally stoic features.

And just to the side of him, I saw Astrid on the ground, an arrow nocked to the string of her bow. She let it fly, and the arrow struck Tariq square in the chest. He staggered back with a cry as Rigel moved to finish him off. Nyra wailed behind me.

And then Astrid restrung her bow and swiveled to point it directly at me. I dropped to the floor in an instant. Astrid's arrow whizzed overhead, embedding itself in Nyra's shoulder. She had been sneaking up behind me while I faced Tariq, so she could deliver a stab to my unprotected back.

The circle beneath us suddenly flickered, pausing near the ninety percent mark. A quick glance revealed Helga and Adelaide locked in a deadly battle of hexes, while Rafe kept would-be interference from some tribesmen at bay.

No wonder Nyra was getting desperate.

Rigel crashed into Tariq. The knight pushed the bigger man back, away from Nyra and me and towards the edge of the circle, where I glimpsed a number of downed tribesmen with Astrid's arrows sticking out of them, like giant desert porcupines.

Nyra stabbed down at me with quick and vicious strikes that chipped the polished stone floor. I dodged each one, and whipped my feet around and up until I had a moment to jump to my feet. Using my momentum, I rained down a series of blows even as I huffed from the exertion.

I needed to end this.

Our blades locked, our breath mingling as we each fought to force the other down. I remembered the taste of her red lips, the scent of the sandberries that had clouded my mind for so long. The happy memory of the way we had danced in the town square and the way she had felt in my arms, swirled together with the red of my father's lifeblood and the feel of his calloused hand in mine as the life left his clear blue eyes.

"Yield to me, Orion," she whispered, her dark eyes locking with mine even as her arms trembled from the strain. "You are too weak to bear the burdens of the crown."

I almost laughed. *Too weak?* Perhaps that had once been true. But after living as Guildmaster Orion for so long, after losing my father, and confronting the magic that I had resented since I was old enough to understand the true cost of granting a wish, *weak* was no longer a word I associated with myself.

Some of those experiences had nearly broken me. But by the grace of the stars and the deep bonds I shared with the friends who had always stayed by my side, I had made it this far. With them, I would make it farther still.

Even now, the family I had chosen was putting their lives on the line to fight for me and for this kingdom. And with Astrid beside me, I would restore Astoria, and make it better than even my parents had ever envisioned.

"I will never yield, to you or to anyone." My conviction echoed in my chest, and I released some of my starlight into the air around us as I spoke. "And even if I falter, I know I will never have to bear that burden alone."

Nyra's eyes, which had softened in her last-ditch effort to sway me, hardened once more. "Your naive and trusting nature will be your downfall. You should have run me through when you had the chance!"

To my surprise, Nyra dropped her scimitar, allowing it to fall to the floor with a resounding *clang*.

"What are you..." Before I could react, she unsheathed a small dagger, which gleamed with a poisonous green tint, from her waist.

"The reason you will never defeat me is simple," she sneered, her eyes shifting from my face to something over my shoulder. "Unlike you, I know what I need to do to claim victory. And *I* never hesitate."

Nyra then threw that dagger straight past me—and into Astrid's heart.

22

Orion

"No! Astrid!" I roared as I watched her fall with Nyra's dagger in her chest.

Time seemed to slow. The terrified expression on Astrid's face burned itself into my mind, carved itself onto my heart. The memory of losing my father to Nyra's blade rose unbidden in my mind. Was I about to lose Astrid the same way I had lost my father? The phantom sound of a clock ticking echoed in my ears, drowning out the sounds of combat all around me.

The edges of my vision turned red as all of the emotions I had been suppressing roared to life with a vengeance. An icy rage shot through my veins like fire, burning brighter with every breath. My magic responded to my panic, welling up from deep inside, in sheer quantities I could hardly believe.

If it were the last thing I did, I was going to get to Astrid and save her in time. On some instinctive level, I knew there would be no coming back from losing her.

"Daring to look away? You are a soft-hearted fool to the very end," Nyra said scornfully.

I felt the heavy impact of her scimitar hitting my arm—and bouncing right off. I slowly turned to look at her, watching as she gaped in surprise.

"How are you..." she trailed off.

I sent up a silent prayer of thanks for the starsteel chainmail the druid smith had made for me. I had been right to take every possible precaution.

I kicked her scimitar so hard that it skidded across the floor, spinning as it went and nicking the ankles of a couple of tribesmen along the way. They fell with a cry as the potent poison entered their veins. Before she could react or come up with some other trick, I lunged forward and hooked one leg behind hers and sent her crashing to her knees. I then leveled my sword at her throat.

I now had her in exactly the same position that she had had me all those weeks ago.

And I would show her the exact same mercy she showed me. None.

She swallowed nervously, and slowly raised her eyes to mine. "Please, Orion. I have to save them."

Tears welled in the dark eyes I had once found so alluring. But I felt nothing but disgust now. I hardened my heart against what

I knew I had to do. No one I loved would ever be safe, so long as this woman was alive.

And I had already lost far too much to her.

"I will save them for you." Her eyes widened in surprise and disbelief. "But I will do it my way."

Before she could blink, I had separated her head from her body. The tiniest of smiles curved her lips. That promise was my final acknowledgement of the little girl who had wanted to save her sister.

Turning, I sprinted towards Astrid's prone form. I swiftly cut down any tribesman foolish enough to stand in my way. Tariq's keening cry of grief when he spotted his fallen lover was abruptly cut off, but I did not spare so much as a glance in his and Rigel's direction.

I sheathed my starsword and fell to my knees beside Astrid. Her face was deathly pale, and her breathing was shallow and ragged. The dagger in her chest bobbed weakly as she struggled to breathe, but I resisted the urge to yank it out. Right now, it was the only thing keeping her from bleeding out. I reached out a trembling hand to brush a strand of black hair from her face. Only the roots of her hair remained a chestnut brown. Darkened veins criss-crossed her skinny wrists, and the dark circles under her closed eyes stood out starkly.

It was clear from a glance that the old druid king's curse had nearly run its course.

But when my hand brushed against her skin, I hissed in pain and quickly withdrew it. The curse was pressing up against her skin, and it had tried to drain my own magic right out of me.

Panic clawed at my throat. The curse would consume any magic I tried to use to heal her mortal wound.

She was under a double death sentence.

And it was all my fault.

I closed my eyes and clenched my hands into fists as I desperately tried to think of a way to save her. The phantom ticking of the clock rang in my ears, making it hard to think. The flecks of blood on her parted lips brought me back to when my father had lain in front of me just like this. The black waves of grief reared up, threatening to come crashing down over my head once more.

There had to be *something* I could do. I could not bear to let it end like this–not after everything we had been through!

My eyes flew open as an idea struck me. "Noctus!"

He appeared at my side within moments. His black hair was plastered to his forehead, and his chest was heaving from exertion, but his eyes were steely with determination. "What do we need to do to save her?"

"I need you to get the manacles off of Nyra's wrists and put them on Astrid."

His brows pinched together before understanding dawned in his eyes. "Understood." He then sprinted back towards Nyra's still form.

Heavy footsteps came up behind me, and I turned to see Sir Rigel approaching. He was favoring one leg, and there were several tears in his tunic that revealed the chainmail he wore underneath, but he looked more exhausted than injured.

"What do you need? Should I aid the wolf and the raven?"

As he spoke, the blood-red light from the magic circle flickered and died. I felt the surge of magic roil around the room, freed from its chains and ready to run wild on all of us. But then it was sucked away from us and towards Adelaide, whose hands were raised and eyes were glowing a bright crimson. I felt relieved. Now I could focus entirely on Astrid.

"No. I am going to do whatever it takes to save Astrid, which means I will be completely defenseless. Guard my back—just like you always have." I gave him a tight smile, which he returned with a bow before taking up a ready stance behind me.

"Save her. But do not even think of leaving us behind to do it." He glanced over his shoulder and caught my eye. "Do not burn yourself out."

I smiled, but was saved from having to reply when Noctus returned.

"Here," Noctus grunted, as he quickly fastened the sealing, corrupted starsteel manacles around her wrists.

Hopefully, it would subdue the curse long enough for me to heal her. I ripped off my tunic and removed my chainmail and undershirt. I gently pulled Astrid into my arms, cradling her head with one hand and draping the starsteel chainmail over her torso with the other. I felt a slight tug on my magic from the curse, but it barely pulled a sliver of magic out of me. Good. It was working. I wadded up the fabric of my tunic and pressed it around the dagger to staunch the blood flow.

I called on my magic, gathering it in my core. I had a feeling I was going to need all of it to pull this off.

"Orion?" Astrid's voice was barely a whisper of air against my cheek.

"I am here. Stay with me." I cupped her face in one hand, and her eyelids fluttered open.

"Is Nyra...?"

"Dead."

Her warm chocolate eyes found mine and held. "Astoria is saved, then?"

"Yes. All thanks to you."

Her lips parted in a soft smile. "I am...glad. I know you will make a fine king, Sterling." She coughed weakly, and more blood flecked her lips.

"Hold on, Astrid. Stay with me." My voice shook, and I pulled even harder at my magic. I needed to keep her conscious, keep her talking until I had readied enough magic to both heal her wound and undo the curse at the same time.

"Take care of...Nova and Castor for me."

She sounded just like my father had when he was saying his final goodbye. That realization terrified me.

"They finished the sandberry antidote you and Adelaide created," I said, encouraged when her eyes seemed to brighten at the news. "Without them and their hard work, we would have been in big trouble tonight."

"Orion," she whispered hoarsely as she raised one trembling hand to my cheek, "There is something I have wanted to tell you...for the longest time."

I placed my hand over hers and leaned into her touch. "What is it?"

"I have loved you since the day we first met." My starlight reflected in her glassy eyes as my glow intensified and miniature stars began to dance in the air around us. "Your courage and kindness shone through, even in a situation...as dark...as ours."

My voice shook as I said, "I love you, Astrid. I am sorry it took me so long to realize it." My heart felt like it was glowing even brighter than my hair.

Her eyes melted into molten pools, and crinkled at the corners with laughter. "I suppose I can forgive you...for being such a dense Guildmaster."

I chuckled softly, even as I reached and reached and *reached* for every last drop of my magic. "I definitely deserved that."

She coughed wetly, and a tear traced down her cheek. "You have always been my north star. I am grateful...that I...got to spend...what little time I had left...with you."

Astrid's beautiful brown eyes fluttered closed. Her hand went limp.

"Though darkness falls..." I tried desperately.

She did not answer.

Her breaths came in shallow, stuttering gasps. I was about to lose her.

It was now or never.

"Do you need me to...?" Noctus asked tentatively.

"No. It has to be me. If it looks like I am struggling, dump whatever starlight and stardust you can find onto me." I was still not entirely sure if I could replicate what had happened the night I had made a wish to save Rigel's life, but now was the time to try.

I gently lowered Astrid's hand to rest on top of the chainmail I had placed on her while Noctus began pulling out from his bag and mine bottle after bottle of liquid starlight.

I closed my eyes, took a deep breath, and called on the last dregs of my magic. I prayed that it would be enough.

"I wish...for Astrid, the light of my skies and the love of my heart, to be restored to complete health, with no wounds, no sickness, and no malicious magical curses."

For a moment, it felt like the entire world went silent, like it was holding its breath. And then the stars responded.

I poured my magic into Astrid. It felt like I had been struck by lightning, with every fibre of my being buzzing with more magic than I had ever attempted to wield at once. It tested my control, trying to break free and run rampant.

I clenched my jaw, as I fought to corral the magic and focus it around her wound. But some of it slipped into the chainmail instead. My mind ached from the effort, and it felt like my focus was being pulled in a thousand different directions.

Suddenly, I recalled something my father had said to me when I had asked him about how my mother had managed to grant so many wishes.

With heart-wrenching sadness in his crisp green eyes, he had said, "She always let her heart guide her. No matter the circumstances, her deep love for her people acted as her north star, lighting the path before her."

Like a dam bursting open, my love for Astrid came pouring forth. Memories played in my mind's eye, blocking out every other thought and sensation. I remembered all of the sunny afternoons we had spent chatting in her workshop, and every late night of nursing our patients back to health together. I remembered the way she had clung to me when we escaped from Khalifon when we were young, and how grateful I had been when she helped me form the guild. And I remembered the way the starlight had silvered her hair and sparkled in her eyes, as we laughed and danced under the stars on the *StarSeeker*. The feeling of my hands on her waist, her fingers in my hair, and her soft lips on mine echoed in my heart, filling it to the brim with warmth and light, brighter than any star.

The magic stilled. And then it settled.

I commanded it to heal her. The magic obeyed.

I guided it through the process, starting from the inside and working its way to the outside. Partway through, I removed the dagger and cast it aside. I pressed my damp tunic against the wound until I knew the bleeding had stopped completely.

By the time the wound had fully closed, sweat dampened my forehead. It had taken more magic to heal that wound than I had anticipated. But I could not afford to stop.

Not now, when I was so *close*.

I pressed my hand against the chainmail covering her, letting out a small breath of relief when I felt Noctus begin dumping liquid starlight over the both of us. And then I turned my attention to the curse.

It roiled like a living thing beneath her skin, and was concentrated like a dark cloud around her core. I was alarmed to see that only a tiny fraction of her magic and her lifeforce remained. But when a wisp of my starlight touched it, it recoiled, as if burned.

Good.

I set to work, turning my starlight to silver fire that burned away the dark magic clinging to my beloved. It fought back, and attempted to feed off of my magic and steal it for itself. I needed more power, but the stream of starlight from Noctus had dwindled to nearly nothing.

I opened my eyes to see scores of empty bottles littering the floor around us and a handful of dead tribesmen at Rigel's feet. Adelaide and Rafe hovered nearby, watching anxiously.

"Adelaide," I rasped. "I need you to destroy part of the roof. Make me a skylight."

"That, I can do." She grinned, and immediately raised her right hand and shot off a stream of magic into the roof. For a moment, nothing happened. But then, it cracked, and whole sections of the roof came crumbling down.

Rafe shifted into his human form and raised his hands as well, his glowing golden magic forming a shield over our heads. The chunks of roof fell to the sides and crashed into the floor.

As the dust settled, starlight filtered down in soft beams. I called out to it, and the scattered light coalesced into one bright spotlight, shining down from the heavens. It struck me almost like a physical blow, sending blistering power through my veins. Even my skin began to glow so brightly that I could hardly stand to keep my eyes open.

I poured it all into Astrid, but it was still not enough. The curse was stubborn and as slippery as an eel. I reached down deep into my core, where my own lifeforce dwelt. Unlike before, I did not hesitate. Astrid had laid down her life for mine. If I had to give up some or all of mine to save her, so be it.

After the loss of my mother, my father and I had always feared and resented the true cost of a granted wish. But now, I fully understood why my mother had chosen to give up everything for a stranger's child.

For a love so great that it sent her back to the stars.

But even though I knew she was gone, I could have sworn I felt her presence all around me. Her phantom hand touched my back.

The stars engraved in my back from years of granting the wishes of others began to burn, one by one, until it felt like my back was engulfed in flames. Starlight surrounded me, so bright and brilliant that I could no longer tell where I ended and it began.

I took every last drop of magic I possessed and granted a wish that I was certain echoed among the stars.

23

Astrid

*F*or the first time in my life, there was no pain radiating from my core. I felt warm. And I felt safe.

I drifted in soft fields of soothing gray that were filled with an endless array of wildflowers. They swayed gently in a pleasant breeze, and the perfume they released was a heavenly combination of honeysuckle, hyacinth, and lilac. The sky glowed a pastel lavender hue in every direction, as if in eternal twilight. And if I squinted, I could just make out the faint glimmering of some stars.

A simple white dress covered me. There were no shoes on my feet, but I preferred it that way. I could not quite remember why; my mind felt rather fuzzy, like it was filled with cotton.

I aimlessly wandered the fields for a time. But no matter how far I walked, I never even glimpsed another soul. Why was I alone? And...where was this place? How had I come to be here?

The last thing I remembered, I was in Astor Castle. There had been fear, and fighting, and pain. But there had been a light, too. I gazed up at the sky as I poked at my memories. They kept slipping through my fingers like water...or liquid starlight.

A star above me brightened, and my eyes widened. Orion! What had happened to Orion? He had been holding me, and shining so brightly that I could hardly bear to look at him.

A whisper of panic chased away some of the fog. I needed to go back to him—I needed to make sure he was safe!

But how could I find my way home to him if I had no clue how I had ended up here in the first place?!

"Hello?" I called tentatively.

Silence.

"Hello!" I shouted. "Is anyone there?"

I could hear my own voice echo back to me, as if I were trapped in a box with walls painted like the horizon. I wrapped my arms around myself, suddenly feeling very much alone.

This place was beautiful. But it was no better than the dungeons if I were trapped here alone. I pivoted in place, scanning the horizon. It looked the same in every direction, even though I knew I had already walked a fair distance.

I looked up once more. I swept my gaze across the barely visible stars, searching for a north star to lead me home. I paused, staring at the star that had twinkled at me before. Was it getting...brighter?

No. It was getting closer!

Could it be...that a star had heard me? I watched with bated breath as the star rapidly brightened, growing bigger as it quickly descended from the heavens.

There was a blinding flash just before it touched the ground in front of me. By the time my vision cleared, the most beautiful woman I had ever seen stood where the star had just hovered.

She had long, silver hair that swayed in the breeze, along with her simple white dress that closely resembled mine. Her ears were delicately arched and pointed at the tips, and she had high cheekbones and rosebud lips that made her seem ageless. Her skin glowed with an inner light, but it was her vivid silvery-blue eyes that really stunned me. They looked just like Orion's.

Her lips curved into a delicate smile, as if she could hear my thoughts. And when she finally spoke, her voice was as rich as honey and as lyrical as a flute. "You have wandered too far from home, young druid."

"Where are we?"

"This is the plane between life and what comes after." She turned her head to look at the distant horizon. "Do you hear its music?"

I focused my attention in the direction the star indicated. I could just faintly hear a melody coming from beyond what I could see. It sounded like an orchestra of harps, wordless singing, and flutes, all playing in a harmony that made my heart ache for *the warmth, comfort, and rest it offered. It was a familiar tune, though I was certain I had never heard it before.*

"I hear it."

The star turned her gaze back to me. "If you follow that music to its source, you will cross over. I imagine your mother is waiting for you there."

My heart quickened at the thought of seeing her once more. I took a compulsive step in that direction, but something held me back. "Does that mean...I can no longer return to the world of the living?"

"You may yet return—if you so wish it. There is someone desperately trying to call you back to him."

"Are you Orion's... Are you Sterling's mother?" The resemblance was uncanny.

"I am." Her eyes softened. "Thank you for staying by his side all this time—even when he did not make it easy for you."

Tears welled unbidden in my eyes and cascaded down my cheeks. This was the person I owed everything to. "Thank you so much for saving me when I was a baby. I do not have the words to express how grateful...and how terribly sorry I am."

Hesperia seemed surprised at my sudden outburst. But then she drew me into her arms. "You do not need to apologize, my dear. I knew what the consequences would be."

"But if you had not used your lifeforce to grant my mother's wish, you would still be with your son." I had to force the words out around the lump in my throat.

How could she not resent me for separating her from her son and husband?

"I do not blame you or your mother for that night. Do not blame yourself, either." She stroked my hair soothingly, and I noted distractedly that it was blonde instead of brown or black. "While I missed them both dearly, I watched over them every night. Our separation was short compared to the eternity that stretches before us still."

I sniffled, wiping at my eyes. "You mean...Sterling will join you in the night sky eventually?" I found the thought strangely comforting, but my heart ached all the same.

"Not just him." Her eyes glimmered with unspoken meaning. "When a star gives their heart to another, not even death can part them."

"What do you—"

A distant star twinkled. She turned towards it and said, "My love calls for me. Our time grows short." She pulled back, only to clasp my hands. "My little star intends to use the entirety of his lifeforce to eradicate the curse that I barely managed to seal. I must send you back before that happens."

Panic clenched my heart in its clawed hand. "No! Anything but that! What must I do?"

"Hold your love for him in your heart and picture his face in your mind. Then simply wish to return to your restored body. I will send you with a kernel of my power."

I hesitated. "With some of your power?"

She laughed softly when she saw the concern on my face. "Worry not, dear one. My might is not limited as it was while I walked the surface. I have power to spare."

There was not an ounce of worry in her glowing eyes, so I nodded. I glanced one last time towards the hauntingly beautiful music, and silently sent my love to my own mother before turning resolutely back to Hesperia.

I recalled how Orion had made me feel safe and cared for since the day we met, and how happy it had made me when he made a guild we could call home. I remembered the way his rich laughter always made my toes curl, and how his blue eyes seemed to see straight to my soul. Despite the secrets he had kept from me, I knew him inside and out, from his sharp mind to his tender heart. Each memory made my heart swell with my love for him, and remembering the night we had danced under the stars made it overflow, like a cup filled past its rim. I pictured his handsome face in my mind, losing myself in his endless azure eyes.

"I wish to return to my restored body."

The last thing I saw before silver starlight stole my senses was Hesperia's soft smile and loving blue eyes.

When I opened my eyes, I beheld the most beautiful sight I had ever seen—far more stunning even than a lavender sky.

My starborn prince.

Sterling's face hovered just above mine. His hair and skin were glowing with an ethereal silver light, and miniature stars danced through the air around him like a living crown. His tender blue eyes, which had been creased with pain and worry, lit up.

"Astrid," he breathed. He was looking at me with the most heartbreaking expression.

"Sterling." I said his name like a prayer.

I reached up and cupped his face in my hand. He leaned into my touch, his precious eyes melting into pools of sapphire. His skin was warm, and felt more real than anything had in the strange place I had just been. I was really, truly back.

"Please, promise me you will never leave me behind again." His voice was deep and husky. It was the most welcome sound I had ever heard.

"I promise." A tear slipped down my cheek, and he brushed it away with his thumb. "I was so scared. But I knew... I knew you would come for me."

Silver lined his eyes at my words. My eyes dropped to his lips, and in an instant, he was kissing me. His lips were gentle, caressing mine as if they were made of glass.

I wrapped my arms around his neck and buried my fingers in his silky hair. I wanted to be closer to him. I needed to reassure myself that this was not a dream, that I was truly alive and safe in his arms. He pressed me against him and deepened the kiss, sending shivers of warmth straight to my core.

Our tears of joy turned the kiss salty. I had never tasted anything sweeter. Not even my wildest dreams had prepared me for this.

I reveled in the feeling of his strong arms wrapped around me. When he gently stroked my hair, I practically melted. If I never again moved from this spot, I would be eternally happy.

He pulled back, just enough to rest his forehead against mine. Our breath mingled as he whispered, "There is nowhere you can go that I will not follow."

"Good." I smiled through my tears. I took a deep breath, and was almost surprised to realize that I felt no pain. The curse was truly gone. "I guess you finally figured out how to grant wishes."

He chuckled drily. "Just in the nick of time, too."

I brushed a hand through his silver hair, marveling at the way his starlight tingled on my skin. When my fingers found his ears, I paused, confused. The tips of his ears were slightly pointed.

Now I was the one laughing. "Your ears are pointed."

"What?" He brought a hand to his ear, and his eyebrows inched up his forehead as he felt them. He looked utterly baffled. "Well, that is new."

My mind flashed back to Hesperia's glowing countenance, including her arched ears. "I suppose you are a full-fledged fallen star now."

Sterling flashed me that lopsided grin of his that always gave me butterflies. He gently tucked a lock of hair behind my own ear. "My ears are nothing compared to yours."

I frowned. "What do you mean?"

He took my hand in his and pressed a light kiss to the back of it before guiding it to my own ear. I felt my earlobe, and then Sterling gently pushed my fingers further. I slowed where my ear usually curved into a rounded shell, but to my shock, my ear just...kept going...and going. I finally discovered the pointed end several inches away from where it should have ended.

My lips parted in surprise as I felt both of my ears, which were now just as long and pointed as any other druid's. I looked down, and was shocked to see that instead of a brittle black, my hair was wavy and blonde.

"I look like...a druid."

Suddenly, Rafe popped up in my field of vision. "That *is* what you are, after all. Cousin."

I gaped at him, even as Sterling grumbled about personal space. "We are cousins? That would make you..."

"Queen Rowena's son. Not that I remember much from before I was captured," he said a little sheepishly.

"Great. Now you look like one of those tree-huggers," Adelaide said with a mock grimace as she walked over.

She held out a shattered piece of mirror for me, and I gasped when I saw the vivid blue eyes peering out of my face. And my ears...they really did stick out from my head.

I only heard a faint whisper of movement before Noctus appeared. "She looks the same to me."

A heavy thud sounded as Sir Rigel smacked Noctus on the back. "And *that* is why Celeste always gets mad when you try to compliment her."

I looked around at all of the precious people surrounding me. A surge of gratitude overwhelmed me, causing fresh tears to pool in my eyes. I could hardly believe we had all made it.

Sterling pulled me in for another hug, and with my chosen family all around me, I finally felt like I had come home.

24

Orion

"Following your meeting with the counselors, you are scheduled to induct the new members of the Knights of the Evening Star and then attend their welcome banquet. After its conclusion, there are a number of new proposals that require your signature to proceed, in addition to the final approvals needed for your coronation." Zale looked up expectantly at me once he finished reading off today's agenda.

I scrubbed a hand over my tired eyes, but grinned at him all the same. It was good to have my assistant back. Fortunately, the night the tribesmen had taken the castle, Zale had managed to slip out during the chaos. He had laid low with his parents, who lived nearby, and therefore avoided being incarcerated with those who had been captured. He had made it his mission to find me, and had passed vital intel to those who resisted their new tyrant—including Rigel. Zale's information had been instrumental in our successful battle.

"And has the peace treaty with the Talahari Tribes been drafted?"

"I believe that is to be the main topic of discussion in your next meeting, Your Highness." Zale flipped back to the first few pages he held. "From what I have observed, several of the counselors object to showing leniency, and are calling for an invasion and subsequent annexation of the Tribelands."

I scowled. "If we did that, we would be no better than them."

Zale nodded. "Eventually, they would rebel. It would only be a matter of time."

I stood from my desk and stretched my sore muscles. I had opted to continue using my own study in the turret instead of taking over my father's library study. There were too many great and terrible memories there for me to properly focus on the present.

"Has construction been completed on that special project?" I asked.

Zale fell into step beside me as I exited my study and began the descent down to the meeting chamber. "It should be finished within the week."

"Good. I want to show the counselors the architectural plans to help convince them."

Zale grinned. "I had a feeling you would say that, so I took the liberty of borrowing them for the day."

"Stars, I missed having you around."

"The feeling is mutual, sire." He glanced at me out of the corner of his eye. "Though I must admit, I am still getting accustomed to your altered appearance."

I chuckled and ran a hand through my hair. Despite my best efforts, it remained a faintly glowing silver. My ears were still slightly pointed, but at least my eyes only glowed when I was using my magic. "You and me both."

We walked in companionable silence through the halls until we reached our destination. Most of the damage from the last several months had been repaired, though there were still noticeable gaps on the walls, where paintings and tapestries had been removed. Even a few weeks later, we were still finding hidden caches of all of the things the tribesmen had been planning to take with them back to the Tribelands.

As Zale opened the door for me, I straightened my dark blue brocade coat. I was still trying to get used to wearing my formal attire again, after so many months of wearing loose-fitting tunics. But I squared my shoulders and swept into the room.

The richly-upholstered meeting room held a long rectangular table that bristled with high-backed chairs. My father had ordered the most uncomfortable chairs he could find to deter meetings from dragging on longer than absolutely necessary. Large windows lined one wall, so that the view of the sky could indicate the time of day for a similar reason.

I strode to the large chair at the head of the table, where my father had always sat. My counselors rose respectfully, and only sat down again once I had taken my seat. Zale took up position behind me. I took a moment to look around the room at the familiar faces. Most had either been imprisoned by Nyra or had hidden outside the castle, but I was glad to see they all seemed largely recovered.

"Although I understand there are many pressing matters that require my attention, I would first like to settle the matter of the peace treaty with the Talahari Tribes," I announced to open the meeting.

The counselors exchanged glances, but it was the Finance Minister who spoke up first. "Your Highness, we have reviewed the draft, and I must strongly recommend you reconsider. You are being far too lenient with the desert barbarians."

Several of the others murmured their agreement.

"What, precisely, would you have me change?" I had already heard from Zale what they wanted, but I wanted to hear it for myself.

"We believe it is only right to demand significant reparations for all the damages we suffered," the Finance Minister said hotly. "To compensate us not only for the physical damage, but also for the damage to our trade, economy, and the loss of life they caused, both directly and indirectly."

The Minister of Defense slammed his fist against the table. "That is not enough! We must ensure that those barbarians can never *dare* pull another stunt like this again! Sire, I believe it is in Astoria's best interest to subjugate the Tribelands, and annex them into Astoria."

"While I understand your frustrations, doing so will certainly incur heavy casualties. And even if we succeed, it will only be a matter of time before they rebel." Several of them started to protest, but I held up a hand for silence. "That being said, I have come up with a plan that will both punish the tribes and eliminate any threat they may pose."

"Surely, you are not considering granting a wish to restore their oases," protested the Minister of Defense.

"Not exactly." I gestured to Zale, and he stepped forward to place diagrams and architectural drawings along the table.

I gave the counselors a few minutes to thoroughly examine each of them before I began my explanation. "As you are all well aware, restoring their oases is not even an option available to us. And yet, without solving the water crisis, the tribesmen will surely continue their invasions."

"So you intend to build them water fountains at our expense?!" The Finance Minister exploded, half-standing from his seat.

"Yes and no." I waited for him to sit back down before I continued. "I am going to gift each of the five tribes one fountain. By combining my magic with druid magic, I will create an artifact that can convert starlight into water. However, this gift comes with strings attached. A barrier will be placed around the Tribelands. It will prevent the tribespeople from leaving their ancestral lands again."

Silence reigned for a beat as the counselors processed this information.

"It is my understanding that the magic of the stars cannot create such barriers. Especially for an indefinite period of time." The Minister of Development stroked his beard thoughtfully.

"It cannot. Which is why, in addition to using the druids' wild magic, we will also be using the magic of a witch."

The counselors looked at me as if I had gone mad.

"Blasphemy!"

"Outrageous!"

"Absolutely ridiculous!"

"Silence!" Zale ordered. Once they had quieted, he continued. "Last night, the Redgrave Coven, under the leadership of Adelaide Redgrave, who aided us in retaking Astor Castle, offered to form an official alliance with Sylvaine and Astoria."

Stunned silence met his words.

"Headwitch Adelaide will create the barrier, and the Redgrave Coven will be responsible for its maintenance." I smiled grimly as I watched most of the assembled faces slacken for a moment before shifting into expressions of careful consideration.

They had taken the bait.

Hook, line, and sinker.

After that little announcement, the rest of the meeting went fairly smoothly. In addition to finalizing the peace treaty, we made good progress on drafting the terms of an alliance with the Redgrave Coven that were similar to those we had already enacted in our formal alliances with Sylvaine and Harland.

I was both thrilled and exhausted. I slipped a hand into my coat pocket and gently wrapped my fingers around the small box there, just to reassure myself it was still there.

Tonight could not come soon enough.

The ceremony went well. Rigel had done an excellent job selecting and training the new recruits, and I enjoyed seeing how thrilled the knights were to accept their new starsteel swords, along with their commissions.

Before I knew it, the afternoon was already over, and it was time for the celebratory banquet. After I gave a short welcome speech, everyone sat down to enjoy the feast at a long banquet table in the ballroom. The throne room was still undergoing extensive repairs, and wisps of malicious magic lingered in its stones. But the candlelight shining off of the polished floor gave the large room a cozy ambiance, especially when it was filled with so many finely-dressed people.

I was seated at the head of the table, with Sir Rigel and Sirius to my right, resplendent in their knightly uniforms, and Captain Jolene and Leo on my left, both wearing the crisp coats of a starship captain and a diplomat, respectively. The more senior members of the knights were seated on their other sides, with the newest members clustered at the far side of the table.

"Congratulations on becoming a knight, Sirius," I said warmly, raising my glass in his direction.

"Hear, hear!" Leo and Jolene cheered, raising their glasses as well.

He grinned. "Thank you, Orion—I mean, sire." He corrected himself when Rigel elbowed him in the ribs.

It would take some getting used to, hearing my guild members using my title. "And how has Estelle been settling in?"

Sirius' eyes softened. "She has enjoyed being back home, and was thrilled with her first starship visit."

"She is welcome anytime. Though if you are not careful, Aria may yet convince her to sign on as an apprentice starbird keeper." She chuckled.

Leo laughed, and placed his hand on Jolene's. Their matching wedding bands glinted in the candlelight. "At this rate, we may well become outnumbered by the starry-eyed younglings."

After everyone laughed good-naturedly, I raised an eyebrow at Jolene. "Have you given any more thought to what we discussed earlier?"

She and Leo shared a glance, before turning to face me fully. "My recovery has been...slower than I might have hoped," she began, her free hand slipping under the table to rest on her left knee.

During the fight to retake Astor Castle, she had shoved Aria out of the way of an incoming attack, and had lost the lower half of her leg as a consequence. Only in the last week had she regained enough strength to begin to walk again, using the wooden leg the druids had crafted for her.

"But once I am fighting-fit once more, I would gladly accept the commission of Admiral." Her vibrant green eyes held mine.

"I am happy to hear that, Captain. I know I can rest easy with you in command of our new fleet." I sat back in my chair and let out a relieved breath. I had been a little worried that Jolene might insist on retiring after recent events. But I was glad to see that her adventurous spirit remained undimmed.

"What are your thoughts on giving starsteel watches to the leaders of our allies to open communication lines?" Leo suddenly asked. He had been taking his role as my Ambassador to Harland quite seriously, and had already paved the way for our formal alliance with them.

"That is certainly worth considering." I rubbed my chin. "Harland could report on any activity from the Tribes or the hostile covens, and request our aid in a timely manner."

He nodded. "Queen Rowena and Prince Rafe also seemed intrigued by the possibility. The wolf-shifter especially."

I smirked. "That does not surprise me in the least."

I exchanged knowing looks with the others. It was no secret that Rafe and Adelaide had been spending quite a bit of time together, despite the misgivings of their respective peoples. They still had a long road ahead of them, but I had a feeling that before long, the druids and the Redgrave Coven would become fast allies. After all, we might see the first Druid King and Headwitch marriage in history.

I was happy for them. They had chosen a path littered with thorns, but if anyone could make it happen, it was those two.

"Will Astrid not be joining us tonight?" Sirius pulled me from my thoughts.

I smiled ruefully. "Unfortunately not. With Noctus and Celeste away on vacation at the lake house, Astrid has been running Hyperion—in addition to teaching her apprentices."

Sirius chuckled. "She is nothing, if not dedicated."

"That she is." I was looking forward to when Noctus and Celeste returned. I had officially named Noctus as the new Guildmaster, and Celeste had decided to stay on as his assistant—and lady.

"So, when are you going to ask her?" Rigel asked coyly.

"I was hoping to ask tonight, but Astrid opted to finish her work at the guild instead." I could feel the tips of my pointed ears turning pink, and to my chagrin, Jolene began poking at the little stars that suddenly formed around me. I was still getting used to how my magic now responded to changes in my emotions. It made it much harder to hide how I was feeling. I slipped my hand around the box in my pocket instinctively.

"Excuses." Leo smirked at my expression. "I think you have made the poor girl wait long enough."

I bristled. "I know. I just...have yet to find the perfect time." I hesitated for a moment. My stomach twisted itself into knots at the thought of the question I was going to ask her. The little box had been burning a hole in my pocket for two weeks, but I had never quite found the right moment.

I let out a breath and squared my shoulders. "But you are right." The others grinned at me, and I glanced at Jolene as I began to formulate my plan. "Can I count on you for help?"

The former pirate lifted her chin cockily. "Can you count on the stars to shine?"

I chuckled. Instead of waiting for the perfect opportunity, perhaps it was time I created it myself.

I clasped Jolene's hand. "Then let us make it a night to remember."

25

Astrid

"What happens if you mix the sandviper venom with liquid starlight?" Aria asked curiously, as she leaned over Nova's shoulder to watch her work.

I continued scribbling away in my notes on the effectiveness of the sandberry antidote at my desk. I had resumed giving my apprentices lessons on herbs and remedies a couple weeks ago, and it made me happy to have my workshop filled with people once more. Aria had been asking many pointed questions, and this presented a great opportunity for Nova to demonstrate her newfound knowledge. It would be good to hear her explain to Aria why those two ingredients should never be mixed.

"Good question. How about we find out?" Nova reached for a vial of liquid starlight.

I froze, looking up in alarm.

"Nova, wait—" Castor tried valiantly to get the vial away from her, but it was too late. I shielded my eyes.

Boom.

I slowly looked up to see Nova and Aria staring down at the bubbling concoction with twin looks of shock on their faces. Nova's red hair and Aria's dark hair had become all frizzy from the reaction. Castor was frozen, half-risen from his seat, his arm still outstretched towards Nova and a look of grumpy acceptance on his face. Half of his blonde hair had been pushed back, giving him a windswept look.

They all stared blankly at each other for a moment. My traitorous lips twitched upwards, but when Nova exhaled a puff of starlight, I could not hold it in any longer. I burst out laughing.

The three teenagers turned to look at me in surprise. Instead of being cross at me for laughing, they joined in, with all three pointing at each other's new hairdos. Nova even pulled some of her hair straight up, so that it stuck up like a horn, before sagging back down. Aria tried to comb the other side of Castor's hair back, so that it matched the windswept side.

It felt so good to simply laugh and enjoy these little moments. I was so incredibly grateful that I had been granted that chance.

"So," I said as I wiped tears of mirth from my eyes. "What have we learned today?"

"That Nova cannot be trusted around anything that could *explode.*" Castor rolled his eyes and Nova stuck out her tongue at him.

"That Castor should style his hair up more often." Aria giggled.

"That sandviper venom and liquid starlight do not mix?" Nova glanced at me sheepishly.

"Correct. And why is that?"

"Um…" Nova bit her lip and glanced at Castor, who sighed.

"Because the magic of the stars generally overpowers all other forms of magic," Castor grumbled, swatting Aria's hands away from his hair. "Especially in large quantities. Also, it tends to explode when shaken."

"What he said!" Nova grinned cheekily.

"Good job, Castor." I turned to Nova. "But Nova, you should have known that too. *And* you should have been more cautious about combining unfamiliar ingredients."

"I apologize." She stuck out her lower lip in a pout.

"Well, as long as you remember for next time, I will not hold it against you." I softened my tone a fraction, but before she could celebrate, I added, "Once you finish cleaning up, you can call it a day."

Nova's expression soured and she glanced at Aria and Castor pleadingly.

"You get to clean up your own mess, Nova. The other two only need to tidy their own stations." I smiled bemusedly as she deflated.

"Fine." Despite her protests, Nova rolled up her sleeves and got right to work. At least most of the mess was contained within her mixing bowl.

A knock sounded at the door.

"Enter."

The door creaked open, and Estelle poked her little head in. She glanced around, her eyebrows quirking upwards when she spotted Nova and her experiment. "Is now a bad time?"

I laughed. "No, we just finished our lesson for the day. What can I do for you?"

"There is someone here to see you!" she sang, and then gave me a wink.

I could only think of one person who would elicit that reaction from Estelle. My heartbeat picked up, and I could not help the smile that bloomed on my face.

"Tell him I will be right there."

"You got it!" Estelle grinned as she left, shutting the door softly behind her.

I ran my fingers through my hair, trying to comb it into a semblance of smoothness. I stood, saying as I slipped out the door, "I trust there will be no more explosions while I am away." I could hear Nova start sputtering indignantly, and smiled to myself.

Hopefully, Nova would finish tidying up properly, even without me in the room. But with Castor by her side, I was sure I had nothing to worry about.

Sterling was waiting for me near the guild's entrance.

He was leaning casually against the wall with his arms crossed over his broad chest, a bemused smile on his face as he chatted with Estelle. He wore his navy blue jacket that was trimmed with silver, instead of the dark, simple clothes he used to wear as Orion. His starsword was belted to his side. Now that his hair was permanently a glowing silver, he had given up on trying to hide who he was.

He laughed at something Estelle said, and the way his dimples flashed set butterflies loose in my stomach. Here was a sight I would never tire of seeing.

"Hello, you two."

Sterling turned at the sound of my voice. When he saw my face, his smile faltered, and his brows pinched together in concern. I paused, an irrational part of me wondering if my changed appearance had thrown him off. He strode purposefully over to me and placed his calloused hand against my cheek. His thumb tenderly brushed the corner of my eye.

"Have you been crying?"

I blushed. *Oh.* So that was what had caused that reaction. I felt silly now for doubting him. "Yes. I have been plagued by nightmares, as of late."

He tensed. "About when Adelaide captured you?"

I glanced down. "Yes." There was little point in lying. I had suffered from nightmares for a time after we had escaped Khalifon, as well. I looked up, and put on a bright smile. "But just like last time, I know that the darkness of those memories will fade, eventually."

Sterling gave me his signature lop-sided grin, and stepped forward to brace his hands on either side of my head, trapping me against the wall. My core heated up as I was forced to look up at him. His eyes softened. He glowed brighter, his magic sending undulating waves of starlight into the air around us. "Then allow me to shine a light on that darkness for you."

I pursed my lips, trying to keep a straight face, but I could not hold in my laughter. "You never seem to run out of star-related comebacks."

He chuckled, even as his eyes melted into pools of sapphire and dropped to my lips. "How could I resist? That one was perfect!"

I tilted my face towards his in silent invitation. "I never said I disliked it."

"Good. Because there is plenty more where that came from."

He dipped his head and brushed his lips against mine, as soft as starlight. When I reached up and wrapped my arms around his neck, he made a noise in the back of his throat and deepened the kiss. He pulled me flush against him, and I smiled against his lips.

When I was in his arms, I felt so safe. Everything else faded into the background, and I could almost pretend that Nyra and everything she had done was nothing more than a distant nightmare.

I tangled my fingers in the cool strands of his hair, enjoying the sensation of his starlight caressing my skin. He held the back of my head so gently, and I shivered at the heady feeling of his fingers sliding through my long blonde hair. His thumb brushed against the arch of my pointed ear, and I moaned.

He drew back in surprise. I felt my face flush scarlet, my embarrassment only deepening when he gave me a satisfied grin. I was still getting used to how sensitive my new ears were.

I suddenly remembered that Estelle had been in the room, and snuck a glance towards where she had been standing. To my relief, she was no longer there.

"Estelle left a while ago. She knows when to make herself scarce." A laugh rumbled in his chest.

"That is a relief." I let out a breath, but made no move to leave his arms. "What brings you to the guild? I was not expecting you."

Sterling brushed a quick kiss to the top of my head. "Do I need a reason to visit you?"

I blushed. "Of course not."

"I was hoping that you might join me for dinner and then some stargazing afterwards. I wanted to show you my favorite spot."

"That sounds wonderful!" We had both been so busy over the last few weeks that we had hardly had a chance to spend more than a handful of hours together at a time.

"I am happy to hear it. Would you like to go now, or did you want to change first?"

I looked down, and realized I was still wearing my old workshop frock. It was littered with stains from my remedy-making sessions.

"Wait just a minute while I change. I will not be long." I reached up on my toes and pecked him on the cheek before darting towards my room. His sultry chuckle chased me inside. I closed the door and turned to face my newly-furnished closet. Tonight, I would make Jolene proud.

About twenty minutes later, I emerged from my room. I had replaced my stained frock with a silvery-blue dress that fluttered when I moved and had tiny pearls stitched into the bodice. The matching shoes had low heels but were quite comfortable to walk in, and I wore the aquamarine necklace and matching hair clip Jolene had given me.

Sterling stood where I had left him. His eyes lit up when he saw me, and I smiled at his reaction.

"How do I look?" I asked a tad nervously as I approached.

"Princess," he said as he took my hand and lifted it to his lips, his clear blue eyes never leaving mine. "You shine brighter than any shooting star."

I smiled. I supposed I could get used to the constant star references if they were all like this. "Thank you, Prince Sterling. You look quite twinkly yourself."

He straightened, raising an eyebrow. *"Twinkly?"*

I grinned cheekily. "You are not the only one who can make references."

His lips curved into a smile as he offered me his arm. "Then I suppose I must live up to your expectations."

As I slipped my arm around his, starlight poured off of him in sudden waves, and miniature stars danced around us. I giggled at the sight, and he sent a group of them swirling around my head.

"I see someone has been practicing," I commented as we left the guildhouse. Calling on my own magic, I paused outside the door and coaxed a starflower into bloom. I plucked the stem and tucked it behind Sterling's ear.

"It appears I am not the only one. Thank you for the gift."

I nodded, and leaned against him as we walked. "Where are we going for dinner?"

"It is a surprise," he said teasingly. "But I promise you will love it."

We strolled along, enjoying the lovely ambiance of a country at peace. We both drew plenty of stares, and a number of people bowed respectfully to Sterling. But it did not bother me as much as it used to.

The streets were not quite as busy and boisterous as they had been before Nyra took over. Too much grief and loss still hung in the air; too many people had been lost for life to resume as if nothing had happened.

But fresh flowers had been planted in the hanging flower baskets, and children ran underfoot once more, laughing and playing games in the warm afternoon sun. The debris that had collected in the streets had been cleared, and those who had been displaced from their homes had returned to them. Now and then, I could hear the faint strains of distant melodies playing, their lively tunes lifting the people's spirits, along with their feet as they danced.

A passing druid bobbed his head to me respectfully, and I returned the greeting with a nod. I was still trying to process the fact that I was the lost druid princess. But it was comforting to know that I had an aunt and a cousin who cared for me in Sylvaine. Though Queen Rowena still stubbornly refused to call me Astrid, insisting instead on Elowen.

The turns we took soon began to feel familiar. Before I knew it, we had left the residential and merchant districts behind. The scent of water and the sound of small waves lapping against the hulls of large ships reached me, and after a few more twists and turns, Lake Hesperia spread out before us. The setting sun transformed the lake into a golden mirror, and silhouetted the docked ships like silent sentinels.

Sterling headed straight towards the *StarSeeker*.

"Since when has there been a restaurant on Jolene's ship?" I could just make out a handful of figures moving around on deck.

"Since about an hour ago." He winked at me. "I hear it is a one-time only, one-night event."

"Is that so?" I hid my smile, touched that Sterling and Jolene had planned this just for me.

"Would I lie to you?" My steps slowed. It took him a moment to realize what he had just said. He grimaced, looking away, and added, "That was not what I meant—"

I halted, and gently turned his face towards me. "I understand why you kept your identity hidden for so long. I always knew you were keeping secrets, but I also knew you must have had a very good reason. And you did." His expression softened, so I continued, "Besides, you were not the only one keeping secrets."

His tense shoulders relaxed, and he leaned into my touch. "For what it is worth, I regret not telling you sooner. But going forward, I will never keep a secret from you again."

"I will hold you to that." I had never felt the need to ask for an apology from him, but it felt nice to hear all the same.

"Shall we?" He held out his arm, and I slipped my hand around his bicep.

Our footsteps echoed on the wooden planks as we crossed the dock and walked up the gangplank. I paused at the top to look across the deck. A small table with two chairs sat near the bow of the ship. It was covered in a white linen tablecloth and topped with place settings for two, along with a pair of tall candles in the middle.

"Welcome to the Pirate's Galley, the best floating restaurant in Astoria," the former pirate announced as she approached. She swept her tri-cornered hat off in a grandiose bow, and I could not help but giggle at her antics. "You both look stunning. Please follow me to your private table."

When he got to the table, Sterling pulled out my chair for me before taking a seat himself.

"The first course will be out shortly. Enjoy." Jolene winked at me before striding off. My ears grew warm.

"I am surprised Sir Rigel let you come without an escort," I said to fill the silence.

Sterling ran a hand through his silvery hair and glanced back towards the castle. "Well...about that..."

"Please tell me you did not sneak out!" Though I had to admit, that was certainly one of his specialties.

"Kind of." He gave me a sheepish smile. "But we are surrounded by the finest crew-turned-pirates-turned-navy one could ask for, so I am not terribly worried. Besides, I wanted to spend some time with you—without guards hovering around us."

What a very Orion thing to say. "At least now, I can protect you too."

I reached with my magic to the waters below us, and called up a stream of water that I then hardened into an icy spear. I let it spin above us for a few moments before I sent it sailing back into the calm waters.

"Well done. I see you have been practicing." A light of approval shone in the prince's eyes, and I grinned.

"Raiden taught me and Rafe a thing or two before they returned to Sylvaine." I smiled fondly at the memory.

Sterling shifted in his seat, suddenly looking uncomfortable. But before I could ask about his strange reaction, Jolene placed bowls of steaming tomato soup in front of us.

The topic of conversation moved on to all of our friends and how they were doing. I enjoyed learning about what they were all up to, and I filled Sterling in on how things were going at the guild. But I was certainly looking forward to when Noctus and Celeste returned, so that I could hand off the reins to them.

If I were being honest with myself, I could use a little break, too. And with my two apprentices learning so quickly, I would not have to worry very much about the guild having a steady supply of remedies.

The main course soon arrived: steak and potatoes. It was delicious, and I was almost too full for dessert, which turned out to be a small slice of lemon cake. Somehow, I made room for dessert as well.

By the time we had finished, the candles were burning low, and the moon and stars had begun to twinkle overhead in the darkening sky. I leaned back in my chair. I could hardly remember the last time I had been treated to such a fine meal. Knowing someone else had cooked it and would clean up afterwards somehow made it taste even better.

Sterling stood, and came around the table to pull my chair out and offer me his hand. "My lady."

"Are we not stargazing on the starship?"

He shook his head. "I want to share with you my secret stargazing spot. It is not too far from the castle."

"Lead the way," I said as I accepted his hand and let him pull me to my feet.

"Thank you for dining at the Pirate's Galley!" Jolene called as we headed towards the gangplank. "Enjoy the rest of your date!"

I blushed, but called back, "Everything was lovely, Jolene. Thank you!"

With a wave, we descended out of sight. Arm in arm, we strolled by the water's edge, laughing to ourselves about Jolene's marvelous performance as a restaurant owner.

After we had circled the castle, we entered a lush forest that backed up against the mountains that towered over us. I paused to look up, awed by the sight. I was also confused: the mountains blocked out half of the sky.

"Are you sure this is the right place?"

"Trust me." Sterling led me closer to what appeared to be a sheer cliff, and helped me step up onto some sort of stone platform. He pulled me close, wrapping an arm around my waist. "Hold on tight."

I wrapped my arms around him as he dipped his hand into a pouch on his belt I had failed to notice, and withdrew a handful of stardust that he sprinkled over the stone slab.

I gasped and tightened my grip as the platform began to rise. It floated up past the tallest trees, so that we could look down on them from above. The rough rock face at our backs appeared as if it were sliding down past us, so I half-turned to look at it, but it continued beyond where I could see.

"We will be higher than the castle soon," Sterling murmured.

I watched as well, as we rose higher than the tips of the tallest towers and turrets. The buildings that made up our home shrank, until they seemed to be the homes of little sprites. After scanning them, I was able to pick out the orphanage's ivy-covered, red-brick facade among them.

"I can see Evelyn's Home from here," I whispered.

"Yes." Sterling chuckled and pointed past it, towards the merchant district. "And if you look there, you can just see the roof of the guildhouse."

I shivered as a sudden gust of wind nipped at my skin. We were so high up that the temperature had dropped quite a bit. I heard a rustle of fabric, and then without a word Sterling settled his coat around my shoulders. His warmth enveloped me, and I hid my chilled fingers inside the sleeves that were far too long for me.

The stone platform shuddered, but Sterling steadied me against him. "We have arrived."

I turned to see that the stone platform had come to a stop so that it was level with the top of the cliff. We were now more than two-thirds of the way to the mountain peak. To my surprise, instead of being a bed of rough rock, it was carpeted with thick grasses and absolutely covered with starflowers. Towards the center was a small pond, with a cluster of lilies in the center, and fireflies flickered around it, creating the illusion of stars on the water's glassy surface.

I stepped forward with Sterling at my side. I turned in a slow circle, taking in the beautiful scenery. "What is this place?"

"My parents discovered it when they first fled here from Harland." He put his hand on my lower back and guided me to the other side of the pond. "They chose to build their new home here because it was the midpoint between the earth and the sky."

"How romantic." I could see why this place would have been so special to two people who were far from home.

"And this pond never changes, even after a drought or heavy rains. My father told me that, whenever my mother gazed down into it, she felt like she was still among the stars."

I peered down into it as we approached the water's edge. It felt like I had fallen into the depths of the sky, and was floating among the stars. Beautiful swirls of deep blues and purples were lined with glittering stars in a never-ending pattern that made me feel small, but at the same time, like I was a part of something grand.

Sterling gently gripped my chin and moved my gaze towards where the stone platform still hovered, glowing faintly. "My father tried to replicate that feeling for her, so she could look down on the lights of Astoria and feel like she was home."

"Was she often homesick?" I had no clue what the life of a star would be like. How much had Hesperia given up to fall to earth? Had she ever missed those she had left behind, or regretted the choice she had made?

I thought back on the beautiful star I had met in my dream. She had smiled so radiantly at me that I could not imagine her features ever dimmed by sorrow or regret.

"Sometimes." Sterling gave me an odd look, and laced his fingers through mine. "But I know my father spent every moment he could by her side, so that she would never feel alone."

"I would like to believe that he returned to her side." I tilted my face to the sky, my eyes settling on the brightest star I could find. A second star twinkled right beside it, so close they almost looked like one.

"As would I." Sterling followed my gaze, and his fingers tightened around mine. I gave him a reassuring squeeze, and his eyes returned to mine. A shadow darkened his gaze. "Astrid. Do you... Now that you have reconnected with your aunt and cousin...will you be returning to Sylvaine?"

I blinked. Was he worried I would leave? A smile curved my lips. I went up on my toes and placed my free hand on his chest. "My home is here. With you."

Something flickered in his blue eyes. "Good," he growled. "Because I would be lost without you, and I have no intention of ever letting you go."

He closed the last few inches between us and captured my lips with his own. He explored my mouth greedily, and when I speared my hands through his hair, he shuddered and pulled me closer. I melted at his touch, my core heating up.

I felt my magic surge in response, and pulse in time with every kiss. Sterling traced a line of steaming kisses from the corner of my lips to the side of my jaw, and I moaned when he hit the sweet spot right by my ear. His cool starlight caressed my skin. Some of my wild magic spilled over and sank into the earth around us, and I did not have to look to know that a whole host of glowing starflowers had sprung up at our feet.

He tucked a lock of hair around my ear, and I could not help but shiver at his touch. He leaned back and raised an eyebrow at me.

I flushed. "My ears are surprisingly sensitive. I...am still getting used to them."

Sterling chuckled. He took my hand and brought my fingertips to the tips of his own slightly-pointed ears. They were warm, and his eyes heated at the contact. "We can get used to them together."

I stilled. There was something about the way he had said that that set butterflies loose in my stomach and made my toes curl. "I would like that."

Sterling stepped back, and I started to protest until he got down on one knee. Waves of starlight danced in the air around him, and tiny stars circled his glowing hair like a crown. My savior looked like a prince straight out of the fairy tales my mother had read to me as a child. He reached into his pocket and withdrew a small black box, and the stars reflected in his clear blue eyes as he slowly opened it. Inside, nestled on a bed of black velvet, rested a silver engagement ring, topped with a blue diamond in the shape of a star.

"Astrid, my skies are dark without you. You are and always have been my north star." He held the ring up to me. "Would you do me the honor of becoming my queen?"

Silver that had nothing to do with the abundant starlight gathered in my eyes as I brought my hands to my mouth. I could not imagine a more beautiful scene than this. My heart felt like it was overflowing with love and hope.

"Yes," I breathed. I loved him so much it hurt. "Though darkness falls..."

"Still the stars find their way." Sterling's eyes glowed with delight, and he gave me a roguish grin as he rose and gently slipped the ring onto my ring finger. He tugged me close, and the last thing I saw before he kissed me was a raven flying towards a pair of stars that seemed to sparkle lovingly from above.

Epilogue

"Are you ready for this?" Sir Rigel stood beside me, looking very official in his new Knight Commander uniform.

"More than words can express." A few months ago, my answer might have been different. But after everything I had been through, I was no longer content to sit back and watch someone else dictate the fate of this kingdom and its people.

This honorable burden and exquisite responsibility…

I was ready to seize it and hit the ground running.

From this day forward, I would write my own destiny, instead of waiting for it to be written in the stars.

The bells began to chime, signaling for the jubilant crowd behind me to quiet down. I half-turned as far as I could while wearing my long and heavy fur-trimmed cape, which was a dark blue sprinkled with pale crystals to imitate the night sky, and waved at my people one last time as their prince.

Trumpets blared as the uniformed guards in front of me opened the grand double doors of the Temple of the Eternal Sky. The copious amount of flowers draped along the edifice of the marble building were nothing compared to the wreaths and garlands wrapped around every pillar and festooning every available surface on the inside. A cobalt carpet stretched from the entrance to the altar at the far end of the temple, which was mirrored by a ceiling painted with stars. Rows of alabaster pews lined each side, and were packed with a multitude of nobles, with some commoners towards the back and my closest friends and advisors seated at the front.

As I took my first step into the temple, the choir began to sing, their voices rising and falling dramatically in the honeysuckle-scented air. Every gaze turned to me and the audience rose from their seats. Each person bowed as I approached them, creating the illusion of a wave rippling through the temple.

I ignored the stares and quiet whispers of those present who had yet to see my glowing silver hair. A small child reached out to try and touch the miniature stars that wafted from me, and I had to resist the urge to smile.

A coronation was a serious affair, after all.

I scanned the gathered people as I made my way down the carpet, in as stately a walk as I could muster. I nodded sagely to the nobles and counselors towards the middle and then front as I passed. I allowed the hint of a smile on my features when I reached Commander Regis and the delegation from Harland, and smiled a tad wider at Prince Rafe and his druid guards, among whom I spotted a beaming Ivy.

Despite the fervent protests of my counselors, I had extended an invitation to Headwitch Adelaide as well, but she had declined to attend the ceremony. She had only agreed to visit me afterwards, out of the public eye so as to avoid any...inauspicious commotions on such a momentous occasion. Though I suspected part of her motivation to visit was thanks to the wolf-shifter in the audience.

I grinned unabashedly when I spotted Noctus, Celeste, Sirius, Estelle, Nova, and Castor. Nova grinned back and winked at me, her fiery red curls pulled back in an attempt at a coronet braid. Leo, Aria, Jolene, and the other starship captains were there as well, each of them looking sharp in their new official Navy dress uniforms.

When my gaze found Astrid's, my expression softened. She looked resplendent in a cobalt gown that glittered when she moved. Her hair had been expertly styled and pinned in place with sapphires and pearls that had no doubt been courtesy of Jolene and her impeccable fashion sense. But it was the star-shaped engagement ring she wore proudly on her ring finger that set my heart ablaze.

The music swelled as I ascended onto the dais and took a seat on the throne, which had cutouts of stars on the high back that hovered just above my head. The very same ones that had once hovered above my father's.

Beside me on the altar, a starsteel crown, designed to look like a cluster of stars with diamonds in their centers, rested on a bed of crushed velvet. I knew the responsibility it represented would weigh far heavier on me than any piece of metal ever could.

"You may now be seated," intoned the High Astronomer as she glided forward, her dark gauzy robes fluttering behind her. The choir's singing faded away as she spoke.

I looked out over the sea of my most treasured friends, allies, and subjects as the ceremony commenced. Her words rang out with confidence and clarity, carrying to the farthest reaches of the temple and beyond. She related the tale of the founding of Astoria, and lauded how far we had come since then—despite the loss of both monarchs and the recent invasion.

As she continued to speak, I methodically scanned those assembled, but my gaze was constantly drawn back to the pair of shining blue eyes in the front row. I could hardly wait for the day when she stood beside me at this very altar in a gown as white as the fresh-fallen snow.

"Sterling Astoria, son of Hesperia and Cedric Astoria, will you swear by the stars to rule with wisdom, honor, and courage, and to put the needs of your people above your own—just as those who ruled before you did?" She reverently lifted the crown from its resting place.

I swept my gaze over my people solemnly as I answered, "By the stars, I swear it." I called on my magic so that I glowed as I made my vow, and starlight wafted into the air around me.

The High Astronomer lowered the crown onto my head, and I allowed my power to fill the crown. Its stars glowed nearly as brightly as their eternal counterparts in the night sky.

"Long live King Sterling!" the High Astronomer declared.

"Long live the king!"

Everyone rose from their seats, as the chant echoed through the temple.

"Long live the king!"

They bowed or curtsied deeply.

"Long live the king!"

As the last echoes faded, I rose from my throne and braced my sheathed starsword in front of me, holding on to its hilt with both hands.

"On this auspicious occasion, and as your new king, I have joyous news to share with the good people of Astoria." I used my magic to help amplify my voice, so that even those outside the temple could hear me.

"The events of this last year have been trying for us all." I closed my eyes briefly, as the memory of my father surfaced in my mind. "But we have come through them as victors—and thanks in no small part to many of you in this room, as well as those whose homelands lie elsewhere. Therefore, it is with the greatest pleasure that I announce Astoria has entered a formal alliance of partnership with Harland, with Sylvaine, and with the Redgrave Coven!"

A moment of stunned silence met my words. Then a few claps and cheers rang out, followed by more and more, until the temple was bursting with the sound of celebration.

Once the crowd began to quiet, I continued, "And after much deliberation and trial and error, Astoria has also entered into a peace treaty with the Talahari Tribes. In exchange for fountains that shall never run dry, not one tribesperson shall ever set foot beyond their own borders again."

This time, the roar of approval was so loud that I could feel it through the stones beneath my feet. I was far from the only one who had lost loved ones due to Nyra's actions, and the stark relief on the faces in front of me told me just how much they had been hurt. I even saw tears of joy, and I had to fight to keep my own eyes dry.

"Going forward, there will only be one Wish Festival held every year, in honor of my late parents." Before any protests could ring out, I explained, "I am pleased to announce that as of today, in partnership with the Hyperion Guild—and as its former Guildmaster—I am opening branches in each district and community in Astoria. I will be granting one trusted individual at each location the right to tap into my power and grant wishes—as needed."

Absolute silence descended, punctuated only by the sound of some people dropping to their knees.

"I would like to take this opportunity to make a confession." I glanced at Astrid, taking courage from her unwavering faith in me. "When I was a boy, I despised wish granting with everything in me. After all, it was the thing that had taken my mother from me, before I even had the chance to know her."

The silence was deafening, and hundreds of pairs of eyes stared at me with undisguised hope and sympathy. "Even so, as Guildmaster Orion of Hyperion, I took it upon myself to save those who did not have the luxury of time to wait for a Wish Festival. And through that work, I came to realize why my mother had chosen to willingly sacrifice her own life to grant the wish of a stranger—and found myself ready to follow in her footsteps." I felt the dark stars on my back prickle in response to the memory.

Astrid's eyes were lined with silver, and I smiled just for her. I knew I would make the same choice a thousand times over.

"Know that the Wish Granters will always be there for you in your hour of need. I expect that knowledge to give you the courage you need to chase your dreams, instead of waiting for someone else to hand them to you on a silver platter." I sent hundreds of little stars dancing through the temple as I spoke.

"Because the best wishes in life are the ones you grant yourself."

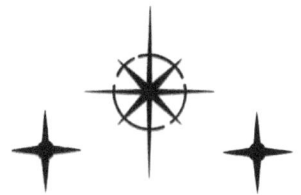

The Adventure Continues...

Adelaide and Rafe's adventure continues in The Witch Queen, which is available on Amazon here.

Reviews

If you enjoyed The Wish King, I would be forever grateful if you would leave it a review on Amazon here! Reviews make such a huge difference, and I love hearing from my readers!

Want Bonus Chapters?

If you would like to order bookish merch, see character art, and receive updates, free book and audiobook announcements, and release notifications for new book, please sign up here:

Also by K. S. Gerlt

The Werewolf's Mask Series

The Werewolf's Mask

Daughter of Wind and Moonlight

Son of Fang and Fury

Daughter of Steel and Strife

Son of Prejudice and Pride

The Werewolf's Mask Series Coloring Book

The Kingdom of the Stars Series

The Starborn Prince

The Druid Queen

The Wish King

The Witch Queen

About the Author

K. S. Gerlt is an award-winning artist and the author of The Werewolf's Mask series. An avid reader herself, she has always loved diving into the magical worlds within books, from the classics to modern fantasy and adventure. She grew up in Southern California, where her pastimes include horseback riding, ice skating, and painting.